To the wide-eyed wonder of children everywhere who, year after year, make the magic of Christmas come alive.

DRAGON RIDERS OF AVRIA

A Dragonhold Christmas

N.A. DAVENPORT

CONTENTS

Avria 
Forbidden Island
Fallshore
Ashfield
Frozen Peaks
Fire Mountain
Morfield
Lightning Cliffs
Hatching Grounds
Aldlake
Poison Plains
Silverlake
Silverpine Forest
Blackstone Forest
N
W
E
S

CHAPTER 1

Corin carefully placed the last link of the shimmering brass chain across the stone wall of the dining hall, taking a step back to admire his handiwork.

"How does that look, Leika?" he asked, turning to his dragon, who was watching from the open doorway.

Leika cocked her smooth yellow head and twitched an ear. *I think it needs to go a little lower.* Her words came to Corin's mind hesitantly, as though the small dragon was putting a lot of thought into her recommendation.

Near the entrance where she stood, a ledge followed the wall where, on any normal day, meals and snacks would be laid out for the young dragon riders. Today, however, festive Christmas lanterns adorned the ledge, casting gentle, colorful glows that danced across the room.

From the other end of the hall, the laughter and chatter of young riders filled the room. Some were hanging boughs of pine, their green contrasting sharply with the dark gray rock, while others strung bright glass orbs, which gleamed like midwinter stars. Every so often, a young dragon would offer its own opinion on the decorations with a puff of smoke or a playful swish of the tail as they followed their riders around the room.

Obliging his companion's suggestion, Corin adjusted the brass chain lower on the wall.

The task of decorating the flapling's dining hall for Christmas was meant to be a chore, a rite for the young riders to contribute to the dragonhold. But, the atmosphere was filled with camaraderie and festive spirit. Stories of legendary Christmas celebrations at Fire Mountain Dragonhold danced in Corin's mind, fueling his anticipation. The transformation of the room, from bare rock to a magical festive cave, filled him with joy. He couldn't wait to see the final result and share in the jubilant festivities every evening.

"Do you know where Dragonlord Brom wants all these clay pots to go?" Rin, a young red rider with short hair that always looked wild, called from the doorway.

Her slight arms strained under the weight of a brightly painted green pot.

"I think he wants them on the tables," Corin said. "They're for the steamed punch."

Rin's eyes gleamed with excitement and a bright smile stretched across her face. "We're having steamed punch? I've only ever heard of that!"

Corin couldn't help but laugh. "That's what Dragonlord Brom said. Steamed punch and blackened leg of bicorn tonight."

Rin gasped. "Wow, I can't wait. My father always roasted bicorn for Christmas too. It'll feel just like home!"

"Really?" Corin asked, pausing as he pulled another brass chain out of the box. "My family never had bicorn. We always had Christmas stew."

"You grew up in Morfield, didn't you?" Rin asked, setting the pot on a table and wiping her bangs back from her forehead. "I hear they have some of the best festivals."

"You bet they do!" Corin said. "The master bard holds a concert in the town square every year. There's a Christmas bazaar where you can buy almost anything you'd ever want!" He hopped down from the chair he'd been standing on and trotted over to her. "And every year there's an epic snowball fight! We build gigantic fortresses out of snow and stockpile hundreds of snow-balls and everything. It's an all-out war! Anyone who walks through the town square is likely to get pelted with a snowball."

There's snow there? Leika asked, giving him a puzzled look and swishing her long tail. Her mind conjured up an image of huge blue dragons flying through the sky on leathery wings and breathing streams of snow that cascaded to the ground in icy flurries.

Corin laughed and rubbed his dragon's budding horns affectionately. "No, no. Sometimes snow falls from the sky without blue dragons making it. Like rain but frozen. Here on Fire Mountain, the snow can't stay frozen because the volcano makes the air too hot. But in most of Avria, there's snow this time of year."

I'd like to see that, Leika said. A hint of longing tinged her thoughts.

"You will someday," Corin said. "I promise." He smiled, a spark of excitement in his eyes. "We'll go on an adventure together and see the snow. We'll make snow dragons, have snowball fights, and I'll bring you to meet my family too. My sisters would love to meet you!"

"It's cool to see how everyone celebrates Christmas here in Avria," Will said as he placed red and gold candles into their stands and arranged them on one of the tables. He ran his fingers through his hair and folded his arms. "It's so different from what I remember back home in Florida . . . I mean the off-lands. Do you decorate your houses and give presents too?"

Corin's friend, Will, was one of the few people who had come to the island of Avria from the mysterious off-lands in decades. No one really knew how people made it to Avria from the off-lands, but it was a strange and mysterious place that didn't have dragons. But they apparently had magical machines that could do almost anything, even fly.

And that wasn't the only unusual thing about the dark-haired boy—somehow he'd found a dragon egg his first year without even trying, and it had hatched into the first white dragon in a thousand years. But Corin didn't see Will as a strange anomaly to be gawked at. Sharing barracks with the other boy, it felt more like they were brothers than anything else. He loved introducing him to Avrian culture and all the amazing things he'd missed out on while living in the far-away realm of "Florida." From delicious Avrian foods to their traditional songs and games. Corin loved seeing the joy and wonder in his eyes as Will experienced these new traditions. And with the coming Christmas festivities in Fire Mountain Dragonhold, Corin knew the best was yet to come.

"Yeah!" Corin said, answering Will's question. He made his way over to his friend and started setting up the candles with him. "We decorate our houses with cedar boughs, pinecones, and red holly berries. My parents used to hide presents for me and my sisters around the house, and the first person to find one would get to light the Christmas candles at dinnertime. My favorite part of Christmas morning was running around and trying to be the first one to find a present!"

"My parents would always hide money in our shoes on Christmas Eve," Rin said with a grin that made the dimple flash in her cheek. "It was great. But Fire Mountain Dragonhold has the very best Christmas Celebrations—not only on Christmas Day, but leading up to it too!"

"The advent parties are so much fun!" one of the other yellow riders chimed in as he helped Rin lift another punch bowl to the table.

"And all the songs and games!" another girl agreed.

"And the amazing food!" Corin said, imagining the steaming hot punch and roasted meat they'd be eating that night.

Corin glanced at Will, but his friend was looking away with pursed lips and a furrowed brow.

Corin gave his shoulder a playful nudge. "What are you most excited about, Will?"

Will blinked and looked up. "Me? Oh . . . " He thought for a moment. "Well, I've never actually seen snow fall before. That would be cool."

Corin chuckled. "You won't see that here on Fire Mountain. But living in Avria, you're sure to see snow, eventually."

Despite Will's answering smile, Corin couldn't help but feel a pang of uncertainty. Was something bothering his friend? Surely no one could be sad on Christmas, though, with the air brimming with holiday cheer and the sounds of festivities echoing all around.

When all the decorations were finally hanging from the walls or adorning the appropriate surfaces, Corin and his friends were free to attend to their other activities. Which, for most of them, meant training for the Dragon Games. The spectacle of their young dragons racing through aerial mazes, striking at gleaming metal targets, and competing fiercely with each other, often drew the residents of the Dragonhold as eager spectators.

As Corin and his friends stepped out of the dining hall, the wide expanse of the courtyard opened before them. Situated over the heart of the volcano, the space radiated with the faint warmth of underground magma, a constant reminder of the fiery world below them.

To their right, the iron doors of the main dragonhold gleamed with intricate patterns, showing the craftsmanship and stories of ancient dragon riders. Directly opposite, and slightly to the left, the barracks came into view. Rows of open archways were carved into the mountain, leading to rooms for young riders and their dragons. The deliberate blend of stone and metal in the dragonhold's construction ensured that almost everything was fireproof, especially against the blazing heat of the red dragons.

As they stepped out into the open space, a heavy wooden cart was making its way into the courtyard. Intricate designs decorated its green and blue-painted walls, with the wheels shining in bright red and the canvas over the mound of goods dyed a brilliant yellow. The hooves of two shaggy shufflos echoed with a rhythmic cadence as they pulled their burden, surrounded by the sheer mountainous walls on all sides. Hunched in the driver's seat, an old man with a wild beard sat guiding the lumbering beasts while a crowd of delighted dragon riders hurried to gather around him.

"Hey, it's a merchant!" Corin shouted to his friends. "Do you want to go see what he's selling?"

I do! chimed in Leika, her claws tapping lightly on the warm stone.

"We don't have any money, though," Anri pointed

out. The young green rider stepped up next to them, weaving her long black hair into a braid at her shoulder. "Jade is ready to start training now if your dragons are."

Corin rolled his eyes. Anri seemed to be the kind of person who always saw the world through a darkened glass. And, in Corin's opinion, the green rider was way too focused on constant training. "That doesn't matter. It'll still be fun to look at what he has, won't it?"

Anri shrugged and tipped her head to the side, conceding the point.

"Let's go see what he's selling," Rin said with a bright smile. "Maybe he's got some things from Silver-lake, Anri. Wouldn't it be nice to see something from home?"

Together, the four friends made their way across the wide courtyard with the older riders. Overhead, excited red dragons swirled and swerved through the sky as they watched the crowd gathering below.

But as they approached the merchant, Corin noticed a fleeting sadness in Will's expression. He looked again, and the expression was gone, replaced by curiosity.

Perhaps he'd only imagined it.

The crowd around the merchant cart had grown thick by the time they made it across the courtyard. Their young dragons stayed back, stretching their necks to watch while the friends pressed through the crowd to see what the merchant was selling.

To Corin's delight, the cart was laden with all kinds of Christmas goodies, clothes, toys, tools, jars of preserved foods from far-away regions, spices, books—almost anything anyone could imagine.

Adult dragon riders from all over Fire Mountain were pushing forward and fumbling for their coin purses.

Will's eyes lit up with excitement, and a wide smile spread across his face as he gazed around at the items in the cart.

"Look, Corin!" he said, pointing to a small box of wood carving tools.

Corin smiled and nodded. "You know, you don't really need money to buy something here," he said. "If you have something valuable, you can always barter for it."

Will looked confused. "What do you mean?"

Corin flashed him a grin. "You just have to find something of equal value that the merchant will accept as payment. It's like a game."

Will smiled, a spark of excitement in his eyes. "So if I had something like a nice pair of boots, I could trade them for a set of tools or a new coat?"

"That's right, if the merchant thought they were worth it."

"Yes, but none of us has anything to barter with," Rin said. She sighed longingly and bit her lip as her eyes slid over a pile of purple silks.

After examining what the merchant had to offer for a moment longer, the four friends finally turned away to let the adults buy their supplies and wares.

"Is there a young dragon rider from Morfield named Corin here?" the merchant called.

Corin stumbled to a stop and glanced around the crowd. How did the merchant know his name? He turned and stepped forward, bewildered, and pointed at his own chest with a questioning expression.

The merchant smiled, his eyes twinkling. "Ah, you must be Corin," he said. "I have something for you; a gift from your mother." He reached into his cart and pulled out a small wooden box, carefully wrapped in white cloth and tied with a green ribbon. Corin's eyes widened in surprise, and he accepted the box with trembling hands.

"Oh, wow!" Rin gushed. "Come on, Corin. Let's get out of this crowd so you can open it!"

"Wait, you're allowed to open it right away?" Will asked, sounding surprised.

"Of course! Let's go find out what's in it!" Corin laughed and bounded out of the crowd.

"I'll meet you out at the training field," Will said, hanging back. "I need to grab something from the barracks first."

"Sure, but don't take too long," Corin called back. "I want to open my present!"

Together, Corin, Rin, and Anri made their way across the courtyard and out to the grassy training field. Their dragons took to the air and followed, circling low overhead and chirping in excitement.

Will wasn't long in catching up to them, panting as he jogged across the dry earth with his creamy white dragon, Vortex, flapping along behind him.

When they were all together again, Corin plopped onto the ground at the edge of the field and pulled the ribbon off of the box eagerly while his friends watched. Inside, his hands first found a new bright-orange linen tunic. He held it up for everyone to see.

"Oh, that's nice!" Rin gushed.

"It looks a little too big," Corin said, twisting his mouth and cocking his head to the side.

"Your mom probably expects you to grow into it," Anri said.

Something in the box smells good. Leika thrust her nose forward and sniffed the box eagerly.

"It does, huh?" Corin wadded up the tunic and set it aside, pulling out the rest of the goodies. A bag of nuts roasted in honey and a pack of spicy shufflo jerky. He held the jerky up for Leika to sniff. "I bet this is what you smell."

Leika bounced on her front feet and licked her lips eagerly. Corin saw the other dragons twitching their ears with interest as well. Rin's red dragon, Ember, made a hungry rumbling noise in his throat and licked his lips.

"All right. Don't drool all over me. I'll share." Chuckling, he passed out a piece of jerky to each of the dragons before sharing it with his friends.

Will leaned against the rock next to Corin, gnawing off a bite of meat. "So, in Avria, nobody waits until Christmas to open presents, huh?" he asked, chewing on the leathery jerky.

"We give presents on Christmas, too," Corin said with a shrug. "But the days leading up to Christmas are also for presents, and you're supposed to open them right away. Why would you want to wait?"

"I dunno," Will said, lowering his eyes. "I guess for the anticipation? It's kind of fun to wonder what's in the box for a while before you open it and find out."

"Is that what you did in the off-lands?" Rin asked.

"Yeah. I mean usually. Christmas is . . . I guess different in Florida than it is here."

Corin lifted his eyebrows curiously. It had never occurred to him that off-landers would celebrate holidays differently than they did in Avria. In fact, he'd never given the off-lands much thought at all before he'd met Will.

CHAPTER 2

"I think it's great that you celebrated Christmas in the off-lands," Rin said, beaming at Will. "I never thought much about what people in the off-lands did before, but it's fun to think that we share some holidays."

Will pursed his lips thoughtfully and then shrugged with a nod. "Yeah, that is kinda cool, I guess. It sure seems like the dragon riders here in Fire Mountain make a big deal out of it, too."

Anri gave an amused snort and pushed herself to her feet. "Honestly, I'm getting a little tired of it."

Corin's eyes snapped to her, and he gave a gasp of shock. "What do you mean?"

"More and more decorations every day. All the festive food they're practically shoving down our throats. They're actually throwing parties every single night! I thought people were exaggerating when they told stories of Fire Mountain Christmas celebrations, but they really do make a big fuss over it. Can't we get back to training our dragons now?"

"But, Anri," Rin spoke up timidly, "we are still training our dragons. The parties are held in the evening. They don't take all of our time."

Anri sighed. "I know. That's not what I mean. I . . . Ugh." She scrubbed her palms over her face, and Jade bumped into her side with her snout. Anri absently gave her dragon's green head a reassuring pat. "I don't know what I mean. It just seems like a lot to me. If there's a celebration every single night, it makes none of the celebrations seem special."

Corin wrinkled his brow, trying to understand what weird sort of logic Anri was using.

Will nodded and stood to join the green rider. "I understand, Anri. And I agree."

"You do?" Corin asked, aghast.

"I agree that we should get back to training our dragons," Will said with a small laugh. "That's why we're out here, isn't it? How about it, Vortex?" He turned his smile toward his dragon.

Vortex perked his ears up, and his amber eyes sparkled with excitement.

"Feel like racing these three slowpokes around the field?"

Vortex shook out his wings and squawked eagerly.

"Who are you calling slow?" Anri challenged with a sharp grin. "Did you forget that Jade is the fastest dragon in the hatching?"

I want to race! Leika said, bounding up to join her dragon friends with fluttering wings. *It's so much fun. Can we start now?*

"All right," Will said, clapping his hands together. "Ready? Set. Go!"

The four young dragons took off in a flurry of wingbeats, zipping through the air like colorful blurs. Red, green, yellow, and white wings flashed over the field as they soared and dove, swooped, and pivoted through their course.

Leika did her best to keep up with Jade and Vortex. But even though she was more powerful than Jade and more streamlined than Vortex, only Rin's dragon, Ember, ever lagged behind her.

It didn't matter, though. The yellow dragon delighted in the game and was always ready to try again.

After a few hours, when their dragons were thoroughly exhausted, Corin and his friends returned to the main dragonhold to prepare for the evening feast.

Back in the barracks room he shared with Will, Corin pulled out the orange linen tunic from his parents and held it up to the light. It had gotten a little wrinkled from being wadded up and stuffed in his satchel, but it still looked nice.

"What do you think, Will? Should I wear it to the feast tonight? It is a nice color, isn't it?"

Will paused in the middle of tying his belt and tilted his head. "Didn't you think it was too big?"

"Aw, who cares? It's from my parents!" He peeled off his dusty cream colored tunic and pulled on the new one. He had to fold the sleeves up, and the hem went down lower than it should, but he tied his belt back on and spread his arms, showing it off.

I like it, Leika said, blinking and lifting her head in admiration. *The orange color looks good.*

"I think so too!" Corin said with a grin.

Will chuckled and exchanged a furtive look with Vortex, but Corin didn't care. The tunic was from his family, and he loved it.

He ruffled a hand through his blond hair. "The orange kinda matches my hair, and my dragon, don't you think?"

"All right, you do have a point there," Will said, folding his arms with an approving nod.

Freshened up and dressed for the evening, they

made their way across the courtyard, joining the other flapling riders in the dining hall for that night's Christmas feast.

The sparkling brass chains adorning the walls added an extra element of festivity to the room. The enormous colorful bowls of hot punch steamed and frothed, filling the warm air with fragrant spiced aromas. An apprentice bard played festive Christmas music on his lyre from the corner of the room while the flapling riders passed around platters of hot roasted bicorn meat and mashed turnips, swimming in rich brown gravy.

"Oh, I love this song!" Rin shouted over the chatter of the crowd as the bard took up a new tune. And with the other red riders at her table, they all started singing:

In this season of great gladness, let us lift our voice.
In thanks for blessings given, and for love that we rejoice.
With warmth and light within our hearts, we welcome in
the night.
And dance and sing with harmony, until the morning light
Oh come all ye joyful, and let us sing with glee.
Of feasting and of revelry, and good company.
With decorations bright, of cedar boughs and silver chains.
Let us bask in candlelight, and celebrate in strains.

. . .

WILL LEANED in and murmured in his ear, "Hey, Corin?"

Corin paused in singing to look at him. "Yeah?"

"What is this stuff?" He scooped a spoonful of soft white mush from his plate.

"Mashed turnip, of course." Corin couldn't help but chuckle. "What did you think it was?"

"Mashed potatoes?" Will wrinkled his nose skeptically.

"Potatoes? For Christmas?" Corin snorted.

Will laughed and shrugged one shoulder. "Okay. I guess you do things different in Avria."

The bard continued playing while they finished their meal. Corin watched Will out of the corner of his eye. The other boy carefully tasted the various foods on his plate as though he'd never tried blackened bicorn and hoppleberry jam before. He didn't seem to know the words to any of the songs, not even to "Winter's Night so Bright."

When the meal was over and the games started, Will didn't know how to play Hot Cockles, Yes and No, or Shadow Buff, though he was quick to learn and did well once he got started. Long before most of the other kids were done for the evening, Will slipped quietly out the door and headed toward the barracks, with Vortex walking along at his side.

"Where's Will going?" Rin asked, following Corin's gaze.

"I don't know. He's seemed a little down today. Maybe he just wants to go to bed."

"I think you should check on him. What if something's wrong?"

"I don't know . . . Maybe he's just tired."

"Corin, you're his friend! If something's wrong, you should ask him about it."

Corin took a gulp of spiced punch while he thought and pursed his lips. He wasn't sure whether Will was upset or not. Probably he just wanted to go to sleep. If that was the case, Corin would be leaving this amazing party and walking all the way across the courtyard and back, just to annoy his friend with questions. That didn't sound like much fun.

Then Anri opened her mouth. "Don't be silly, Rin. Will can handle his own problems. And he obviously wants some time to himself. If he wanted to talk to someone about it, he would."

Corin nearly choked on his mouthful of punch. Anri was agreeing with him? Then he had to be wrong. That girl was always abrasive and rude. If her thoughts were aligning with his, he had to be missing something.

"You know what? I *will* go talk to him," he said, firmly placing his mug on the table. "He might need a friend to be there for him when he's feeling down."

"Oh, good!" Rin said, smiling at him so broadly the little dimple in her cheek flashed.

Corin grinned back at her. His grin turned a little smug when he noticed Anri roll her eyes at him.

He gave a determined nod, then trotted out the door.

The moment he was outside, with the chatter of lively conversations and warm, playful music fading behind him, he sighed.

Two curious, shining eyes blinked at him from the dark, then Leika flapped over in a gust of dusty wind. She yawned hugely, showing her sharp white teeth, then bumped her head against him, begging for ear scratches. *You don't want to leave the party. So why are you?*

"You missed the conversation, huh? Sleeping on the basking rocks again, weren't you?"

They're warm and comfortable. And also closer to you when you're in the dining hall.

Corin's heart swelled at his dragon's unwavering devotion, and he gave her an extra scratch between her budding horns. "Yeah, I'm going to the barracks now to talk to Will. Rin seems to think he's unhappy and needs a friend to talk to."

Leika turned her eyes to the barracks and swiveled her ears forward. *He is a little unhappy. But Vortex doesn't seem worried about it.*

"He is?" Corin raised his brows in surprise. He often forgot that the dragons could read the emotions of people around them. He usually just assumed people saw everything the way he did, so why bother asking Leika what they were feeling? "Well, let's go find out why. Maybe he really didn't like the mashed turnips or something."

They found Will sitting on his cot with Vortex's head in his lap, stroking his dragon's eye ridges and nose.

He looked up as Corin entered with Leika walking at his side. "Hey, Corin. Vortex told me that you and Leika were coming to talk. What's up?"

"Oh, well, you know . . ."—Corin waved his arms casually and flopped onto the cot next to Will, eyeing the quiet empty room around them—"I just felt like taking a stroll and thought I'd come see if there was a better party out here in the barracks. You know, where it's all dark and quiet with no food and nobody else is here."

He laughed at his own silly joke and Will chuckled along with him.

"Seriously, though. Why come out here?" he asked. "The party is on fire in the dining hall. We were about to play candy bauble and everything!"

Confusion flashed over Will's features, followed by a resigned frown. He shrugged his shoulders and cocked his head.

"Leika says you're feeling sad," Corin pressed, still not wanting to believe it was possible.

"Well, I am, kinda."

"What? At Christmastime? Why?"

"It isn't—" Will cut himself off and shook his head, giving Vortex an extra pat behind the ears. "It doesn't feel like Christmas to me. I mean, the parties are fun and everything. But I miss my home, my old friends, the way Christmas feels at my Uncle John's cabin by the lake in Massachusetts . . . I mean, back in the off-lands . . . you know?"

"Wait, I thought you came from the land of Florida," Corin said.

"I do, but my uncle's house is up north. We used to always fly up for Christmastime and stay at his cabin by the lake. We'd go to church on Christmas Eve for a candlelight service and sing Christmas carols. We sometimes even woke up to snow on Christmas morning. It never snowed at my house."

Corin was about to ask how they flew somewhere without dragons. Was it really true they had machines that could fly? But Will kept going.

"I know you all have your traditions here in Avria. And they're great, really. But all the celebrating here in Fire Mountain Dragonhold just reminds me of the things I'm not doing back home with my family."

"Like what? What kinds of fun things did you do that we don't do here?"

Will thought silently for a moment before answering. "Well, the food is different, for one. You all have hot spiced drinks, roasts, sweet puddings, and stuff like that. We always had sugar cookies, eggnog, gingerbread, candy canes . . . And for Christmas dinner, we'd eat turkey or a big ham and pumpkin pie."

"I don't even know what most of those things are." Corin could feel his mouth watering even though his stomach was already full. He leaned forward eagerly. "What else?"

"The songs here are all different, too. I don't know any of them. Some of the music sounds the same, but then the words are all different. Nobody here sings 'Jingle Bells,' 'Joy to the World,' 'Hark the Herald Angels Sing,' or 'Oh, Christmas Tree.'"

"Christmas tree? What's a Christmas tree?"

Will laughed and leaned back against the wall.

Vortex lifted his head and blinked sleepily at his rider.

"That's another thing. The decorations are all kind of close to what I remember. But they're all different too. A Christmas tree is a pine tree, like the ones lower down on the mountain. You chop one down and stand it up in your house. Then you decorate it with colorful ornaments and electric lights."

"Electric lights?" Corin glanced at Leika, wondering if his electric dragon had some sort of secret light-making ability he didn't know about. "Why do you do that? And how?"

Will chuckled and raked a hand through is hair. "In the off-lands, people can make electricity without yellow dragons. And they use it for all sorts of things." He paused, scratching his head. "But, why do we put lights on Christmas trees? Honestly, I don't have a clue."

He shrugged and added, "It's really beautiful, though, and it doesn't even feel like Christmas until the tree is up. We put our gifts under the tree and open them all up on Christmas morning." He sighed, and seemed to be picturing the scene in his mind. "Well, not all of them. We put some of the smaller ones in stockings too."

"What? Now I know you're just messing with me! In stockings?" Corin narrowed his eyes skeptically.

Will laughed. "If I really wanted to mess with you, I'd tell you all about Santa Claus, his magic elves, and his flying reindeer!"

"Come on! I'm trying to be serious here!" Corin said, laughing along with Will.

"Oh, I'm not even kidding! Santa Claus is supposed to be a magical old man with a white beard and a big belly. He wears a red suit lined with fur and visits everyone's house on Christmas Eve in his sleigh pulled by flying reindeer. He's supposed to bring presents to all the good children of the world. Some presents go under the Christmas tree, and some go in giant stockings that we hang over the fireplace."

"And you don't open any presents until Christmas morning?" Corin said, remembering Will's confusion earlier in the day.

"Usually not. In my family, sometimes we'd open a present the night before, but that would always be new Christmas pajamas to sleep in."

"Wow . . ." Corin sat in silent thought for a moment. "That all sounds wonderful, really. A little silly, but sometimes silly is fun. I wish I could go to the off-lands and see it for myself."

"I think you'd really like it," Will said with a longing

sigh. He ran his hand down Vortex's neck and gave his dragon's shoulder an affectionate pat. "But I don't think bringing dragons to the off-lands would work very well. Maybe you'd have to disguise Leika as a flying reindeer." He snorted a laugh.

What is a reindeer? Leika asked.

"I have no idea what a reindeer is," Corin said. "Probably something like a bicorn with wings."

At that, Will laughed even louder.

CHAPTER 3

The flapling dining hall was abuzz with activity as the young riders worked to clean up after breakfast the next day. The scent of freshly baked bread and sweet jams still lingered in the air, and the sound of clattering dishes echoed throughout the room.

"So, did you talk to Will?" Rin asked, coming alongside Corin to collect the bowls.

"Yeah," Corin said as he wiped the last of the crumbs off the table with a cloth. "He said he's sad because he misses the way Christmas is in the offlands."

"Oh?" Rin paused in stacking bowls to look at him with an arched brow.

"Apparently, the way we do Christmas in Avria is

29

very different from the way he describes it. But I don't know why that would bother him so much. Christmas here on Fire Mountain is awesome."

Rin shook her head and put a hand on his arm. "No, Corin. You don't understand. The best part about Christmas celebrations is the anticipation. You expect things to be a certain way, and you build up that excitement. Then, when it actually happens, it's so much better."

He furrowed his brow, considering her words, then shook his head. "I still don't get it."

"Well, imagine if you were expecting to have a sweetbread after dinner. You were thinking all through the meal about the soft, steamy inside and the crispy, sweet crust. You could hardly wait for the honey-sweet flavor to fill your mouth . . ."

Corin licked his lips. "Yeah?"

"Then how would you feel if you bit into it, and it was actually a meat bun?"

Corin frowned and wrinkled his nose.

"Meat buns are good," Rin pointed out, "but they're disappointing if you're expecting a sweetbread."

Anri stepped up to them and started stacking the bowls they'd been ignoring. "If what you want is a sweetbread and what you get is a meat bun, you should just enjoy the meat bun, right?"

Corin stacked the rest of his bowls into Anri's growing tower and folded his arms. "Or we could make Will a sweetbread!"

Both girls stared at him, bemused.

"Corin, the sweetbread was just a metaphor . . ." Rin started.

"I know. That's what I mean. We should make Christmas the way Will wants it. We should have an off-lander Christmas party!"

Anri's mouth fell open in an unreadable expression. Shock or awe, Corin couldn't tell.

Rin blinked and gasped, grabbing his arm again in excitement. "You think we could?"

"Why can't we? Will told me all sorts of things he misses about the off-lands. A lot of them sounded like fun. We could have a party and do all those things to help him feel at home."

"Maybe we should ask Will if he wants—" Anri started.

"We should surprise him!" Corin blurted. "Surprise parties are always the best! Can you imagine the look on his face when he sees a real Christmas tree and stockings filled with presents?"

Anri sighed and hauled the stack of bowls over to the wash bin.

"Christmas tree? Stockings?" Rin asked, eyes sparkling.

"I know! He told me all kinds of things that I've never heard of before!" Corin said.

"This is amazing, Corin! We have to do it! You should write down a list of things for the party. Ember and I will help however we can."

"We'll help too." One of the red riders, Dilin came up to them, followed by some of the other kids in the red wing. "We heard you talking. Throwing an off-lander Christmas party sounds great."

"I think we should get permission to hold it in the great hall," Timmin, the smallest and youngest red rider said. "That'll help keep it a surprise."

Jayda, a rider in the blue wing, also joined the group. "Tundra and I will help too. I'd love to learn more about how off-landers do Christmas. What's the plan?"

"I don't exactly have a plan yet," Corin said, rubbing the back of his neck. "Will talked a lot about the food, songs, and decorations. He really seemed to put a lot of emphasis on having a Christmas tree. Oh, and having snow seemed important too."

"The red wing can take charge of the food," Rin offered with a grin.

"Yeah!" the other red riders cheered.

"You said snow was important?" Jayda asked,

exchanging a glance with Beck. The two blue riders nodded together. "Leave that to the blue riders. Our dragons can make it snow for you."

"Perfect!" Corin said. It was all coming together. With the ice powers of the blue dragons making snow, it was for sure going to feel like Christmas for Will. "I'll focus on getting a big Christmas tree with lights and lots of decorations."

"You might want to keep it simple, though," Anri warned, walking back across the room from the wash basin. "Why not focus on a couple of things and make sure you get them right, instead of trying to do everything. Your plans might fall apart if you go too crazy with them."

"Are you going to help or not?" Corin asked, folding his arms and frowning at her doom and gloom attitude.

Anri rolled her eyes. "Of course, Jade and I will help however we can. Will is my friend too, you know."

"Then don't be so pessimistic all the time! This is going to be great. You'll see."

"Fine." She sighed and rolled her eyes again. "I'll talk with Bard Nestar and see if he knows any Christmas songs from the old days."

"Why old Christmas songs?" Corin asked.

"Because there used to be a lot more off-landers in Avria in the old days. If we can find Christmas songs that were popular when our grandparents were born, they might come from the off-lands."

"Oh . . . Hey, that's actually a good idea!"

"Here. I have a blank scroll," Beck said, pulling rolled paper and a pen out of his belt pouch. "Let's write a list of things we all want to do."

"Great!" Corin took the scroll and started jotting down everything he could remember from his conversation with Will. It was disjointed and messy, and he wasn't quite sure he remembered everything right, but most everyone agreed that it sounded like fun, and that's what mattered.

In the end, the red wing chose to focus on preparing the Christmas food that Will had described. They were the most eager to try their hands at making sugar cookies, gingerbread, and candy canes.

The blue riders promised that their dragons could make it snow. Maybe not out in the open courtyard, though. Their dragons were still young, and the hot air of Fire Mountain made it difficult for the frost to stay frozen. But if they all worked together in the great hall, they could probably get the temperature down enough for a nice shower of snowflakes.

Anri was the only green rider participating in the scheme, but she promised she'd do her best to find authentic off-lander Christmas music for the bard to play.

The other yellow riders joined in too, offering to find plenty of decorations. They even suggested having Dragonlord Brom dress up as Santa Claus, the off-lander version of Father Christmas, and get him to pass out presents for everyone. Corin loved the idea and left it to them to convince the Dragonlord to go along with it. They even started talking about dressing the dragons up like flying reindeer or hiring a herdsman to bring a small herd of bicorns up the mountain for the occasion. Then when the party was over, the dragons could have a bicorn feast! Corin thought that might be going a bit far, but he'd let them handle their own tasks.

As for himself, Corin decided that he and Leika should be the ones to get a huge pine Christmas tree covered in ornaments and ready by Christmas morning. All he had to do was find a good tree, make colorful ornaments, and find a way to put lights all over it. That last part might be the biggest challenge, he thought, but he'd focus on it when he got to it.

THE NEXT DAY, after training for the Dragon Games with his friends, Corin donned his sturdiest boots, grabbed his warmest coat, and borrowed a large burlap root bag from the mess hall. While Will was engrossed in one of his "discussions" with Anri, the kind of discussion that often ended with Will flat on his back under Anri's staff or training sword, Corin jogged out of the dragonhold towards the ice-frosted foothills with Leika flapping along beside him.

Are we going to get a tree today? his dragon asked, circling him with lazy beats of her yellow wings. *It will be very beautiful with decorations and lights. I want to see it.*

"We probably won't be able to do it today. I just want to see if we can find a good one. And maybe we can find supplies to make ornaments too. We still don't know where the tree is going to go. And depending on which one we choose, it might be really heavy."

If it's heavy, I can help you carry it. You are very strong. And I'm getting stronger every day!

"I know you are," Corin agreed, grinning up at Leika as she swooped in the air. "But you only think I'm strong because you remember me carrying you around when you were tiny. You're bigger than I am now. You know that, right?"

Leika gave a little snort and dropped to the ground, shuffling her wings against her back. *I think you can still carry me. You should try.*

"Not a chance, you big yellow beast!" Corin laughed and started trotting ahead faster.

Leika lolloped after him, tail swishing with excitement. *You can! I'm not too heavy. I'm only a little bigger than you are.*

Corin turned to ward off his playful dragon, only to have her collide with him, knocking him over. Together they rolled down a grassy hill, shouting and squawking, until they came to a big lump in the ground. Corin ended up face down on the ground with Leika perched on his back, her claws carefully drawn away from his flesh.

See? I won't crush you, she said smugly. *You are strong enough to carry me.*

"Mmmrf! Geroff!" Corin grunted, wiggling his shoulders.

Leika obliged, daintily stepping down to the ground and shaking the frosted grass from her wings and tail.

"You didn't get hurt, did you?" Corin asked, brushing the dirt from his face.

No, I'm not hurt.

"No? Good." Corin grinned mischievously. "Because I'm gonna get you for that!" He jumped on her and wrestled her to the ground, scratching her neck right where he knew she was the most ticklish.

Leika let out a loud squawk and growled fiercely,

sending bolts of electricity crackling to the ground before she forcefully pushed Corin away. The electric jolts passed right over Corin without him even feeling them. Being a yellow rider had its benefits.

Just as Leika was about to lunge at him again with bright electricity crackling along her wings, Corin called out, "Wait, look over there!"

The dragon paused and turned her attention towards the edge of a sparse pine forest. Dry pinecones littered the ground beneath the dark green trees, and at the bottom of the slope stood a well-shaped pine tree with thick, sturdy branches all around. It was the perfect Christmas tree!

CHAPTER 4

Corin grinned. "Look at that! It would make a perfect Christmas tree, don't you think?"

Leika nodded and made an approving rumble deep in her chest.

Together they walked down the hill and circled the bushy tree to inspect it more closely. It was a broad-based fir with fragrant needles and sturdy branches—the ideal tree to hang decorations on.

What kind of decorations will you use? Leika asked.

"Hmm, good question. I guess as long as they're brightly colored, it doesn't matter what we use. Oh, I know! We can paint these pinecones! There are hundreds of them around us, and they're just the right size," Corin said, waving his hands around at the frosted pinecones littering the ground.

Leika fluttered her wings and squawked in excited agreement, the sound cutting through the crisp mountain air.

Together Corin and his dragon got to work, gathering pinecones from the forest floor. Corin tossed them into his bag as quickly as he could while Leika gently gathered as many as she could fit into her mouth and dropped them into a burlap sack as well. Though she left a good amount of slobber on the pinecones, Corin didn't complain, happy to have his dragon's help with the task.

Once the sack was full, they hauled it back to the dragonhold, ready to turn their collection of pinecones into festive decorations for their Christmas tree.

As they entered the courtyard, Leika settled down to nap on a warm volcanic rock while Corin went inside the main hall to search for Tumi. Hopefully, the flapling trainer would know where to find some bright paint to color the pinecone ornaments. But instead of Tumi, he ran into Timmin, the youngest rider from the red wing, who was making his way out of the conference hall. Timmin's eyes shone with excitement as he greeted Corin.

"Oh, Corin! I'm glad I found you," he said.

"Hey, Timmin. What is it?" Corin asked.

"I just spoke with Dragonlord Brom, and he gave us

permission to use the great hall for Will's Christmas party! He said it was a fantastic idea," Timmin said, beaming with pride.

"Really? That's amazing news!"

Just then, Dragonlord Brom himself appeared, his boots clacking on the stone floor as he made his way over to them. He pulled at his beard with a thick, calloused hand and smiled down at them. "Corin, my boy! I hear you're planning a surprise off-lander party for Will."

"Yes, Dragonlord Brom. Can we really use the great hall for the party?" Corin asked, clutching his hands together.

"Of course! It's the biggest room, and the whole dragonhold should be invited. An off-lander party is a splendid idea! You're being a good friend by thinking of Will and including him. If there's anything else you and your friends need for the party, don't hesitate to ask."

Corin beamed up at Dragonlord Brom. "Really? Well, actually, there is one thing. I need some bright paint to make ornaments for the Christmas tree." He lifted the lumpy burlap sack. "Is there any in the dragonhold that I can use?"

"A Christmas tree?"

"Yeah. In the off-lands, they bring pine trees into their houses and hang ornaments on them for Christmas. Will said it was one of his favorite parts of the holiday."

The Dragonlord raised his bushy brows in interest. "Is that so? Then we'd better make sure we have one. I believe you'll find some paint in the storage room behind the shufflo enclosure. Aleri, the instructor for the blue wing, has been using it to create artwork in her free time. She can show you where it is."

"Thank you, Dragonlord. I'll go find her right away."

Corin swung the sack of pinecones over his shoulder and lugged it back outside and through the courtyard, beads of sweat forming on his forehead. He was on the hunt for Aleri, but before he could reach the other side, Beck appeared, trotting across the courtyard and waving wildly to catch his attention. His blue dragon, Icicle, flapped alongside him.

"Corin! There you are!" Beck called.

Corin wiped his brow and rested the sack of pinecones on the ground. "Hey, Beck. What is it?"

Beck caught up to him, and Icicle landed in a small flurry of chilly wind. "I was just thinking, everyone else is so busy getting ready for the party, but the blue dragons are only going to be making snow. I'm sure we can do something more to help."

Corin raised his eyebrows. "Like what?"

"Well, Icicle has been practicing making ice formations. Some of them are really impressive—crystalline and sparkly, like snowflakes but a whole lot bigger. We could use them as centerpieces for the tables. I think it would be a nice touch," Beck said, patting Icicle's neck affectionately.

Corin beamed at the blue rider. "That's a great idea! You should definitely do that." He turned to Beck's dragon. "Thank you, Icicle. It'll be a great addition to the decorations."

Icicle gave a soft happy squawk, lifting his head proudly.

"By the way," Corin added, "have you seen Aleri? She's supposed to know where the paint is that I can use to make ornaments."

"Oh, I know where the paint is. In the storage room. Come on. I'll take you there."

Corin gratefully followed the other boy out behind the shufflo pen to a room carved into the mountain wall that was really more of a cave with a door built into it.

They entered and Beck rummaged around looking for a lantern to light. "Aleri likes to make paintings. I've seen her come out here to get her supplies. The paints are in a powder form, and all you have to do is add a little water to get them ready. Ah, here we are." He pulled a lantern down and used a match to light it.

Warm orange light flickered to life, illuminating a

long room lined with shelves, crates, and deep wooden chests covered in a fine layer of dust.

"See the jars all along these shelves?" Beck gestured to the row of shelves nearest to the door. "They have the powdered pigments. Just make sure you don't mix different colors together, or Aleri will get mad at you." He gave a grin that looked a little sheepish, and Corin wondered if the other boy knew that bit of information from personal experience.

Corin grinned back at Beck, nodding in understanding. "Thanks for the heads-up. I'll make sure not to mix them."

Satisfied, Beck left Corin to his own devices, and he started scanning the shelves filled with jars of fine powder, most labeled with their respective colors.

Some were completely blank, though, and Corin had to lift their lids and look inside to figure out what color they contained. Most of the jars were very small too—scarcely bigger than a kaffa mug. So even when he found a color, like vibrant red, that would work well, there wasn't nearly enough of the powder to make paint for all the pinecones. He would probably have enough paint if he used up all the colors available. But somehow he thought that using up all the paint would irritate Aleri more than mixing two colors together would.

Corin continued scouring the storage room for a while, searching for any missed jars of paint. He stumbled upon a chest of leather dragon-riding gear and goggles, boxes of red candles, and even a rack of cookware. As he sifted through the crockery buried in the back of the room, he let out a whoop of joy when he found a huge crock brimming with a vibrant-yellow powder. "Perfect!" he exclaimed, laughing in delight. He hauled the heavy stoneware crock out of the corner and removed the lid. There was plenty of yellow powder inside for as many pinecones as he could possibly want to paint.

Since he wanted to keep his project hidden from Will until Christmas, Corin decided to stash his project in the storage room on a nearby empty rack. He filled a bowl with water and mixed in the yellow powder until he had a thick pasty paint.

As he mixed the yellow concoction, an unpleasant aroma started wafting up from the bowl. Corin wrinkled his nose at the stink. Did paint always smell so bad? But despite the putrid smell, which reminded him of the stench of rotten eggs, he smeared the mixture over as many pinecones as he could, spending hours perfecting the ornaments and setting them on the empty shelf to dry.

Eventually, Leika stirred awake. *Are you done*

painting yet? I'm so hungry I could eat a whole shufflo, she grumbled groggily.

Apparently, it was time to take a break from his project and tend to his dragon's dinner.

"All right, Leika. I'm coming," he said, resting one more smelly yellow pine cone on the shelf. With a sigh he left the storage room, hoping the unpleasant odor of the paint would vanish when it dried.

CHAPTER 5

In the days leading up to Christmas, Corin focused on preparing as many pinecones as possible. He and Leika made several trips to the forest to collect more, and Corin spent every evening smearing the smelly yellow paint all over them.

He helped the other flapling riders with their party preparations whenever he could, as well. Rin approached him with questions about Will's preferences for the Christmas dishes she was preparing with the other red wing kids. One recipe called for a lot of spirits, which kids rarely drank in Avria. Did off-lander Christmas punch really have so much firedew in it? And what on earth was nutmeg? Corin's best guess was to follow the recipe as closely as possible, and he thought that sablenuts might be a good substitute for nutmeg.

Another red wing girl asked Corin for advice on how to prepare the orange buttergourd for her pie. Since Avria didn't have pumpkins, buttergourd seemed like the best substitute, but different recipes had conflicting instructions on how to prepare the dish. Should she roast it first or cut it into chunks like apples? And should she peel it first? Corin thought it would be silly to cook the gourd first, since it would be baked into the pie again, anyway. And while nobody in Avria made pies out of buttergourd, he thought cutting it up like apples made sense.

The other kids in the yellow wing approached him as well, asking whether their little wooden carved reindeer looked right and how big the red woolen stockings ought to be. Corin had no idea how to answer their questions, but he figured they should do their best to make the stockings as big as possible and have the reindeer look like bicorns with branching horns and wings, since they were supposed to be able to fly.

With only two days left until Christmas, Anri and the resident bard Nestar pulled Corin aside so he could hear the songs they'd been working on.

"There aren't many off-lander Christmas songs in the archives," Anri said, scratching Trouble, her little furry kisnit, behind the ears.

The bard nodded, carefully tuning the strings of his

mandolin. "Regardless, I think we've managed to get a close approximation to a few of them. We have 'The Friendly Beasts,' 'Silent Night,' and 'Christmas Tree.' Shall I play them for you?"

Corin grimaced to himself at the mention of "Christmas Tree," remembering that he still needed to collect the tree and somehow carry it all the way to the great hall without Will catching him at it.

"Is there a problem with that one?" the bard asked with a slight frown on his weathered face, noticing Corin's expression. "I can play something more traditionally Avrian, if you prefer."

"No, no. It's fine. I was thinking of something else. Let's hear it. I'm sure it'll be great."

"Wonderful! I spent a great deal of time restoring the lyrics and melody of this song from the archives. I hope you enjoy it." Nestar cleared his throat and strummed his instrument, then began to sing:

> *Oh, Christmas Tree, oh, Christmas Tree,*
> *How lovely are thy branches?*
> *Oh, Christmas Tree, oh, Christmas Tree,*
> *How pleasant is thy fragrance?*

In winter's chill, we bring thee home,
And decorate thee as our own.
With every painted ball and star,
Thou shinest bright from near and far.

Oh, Christmas Tree, oh, Christmas Tree,
How lovely are thy branches?
Oh, Christmas Tree, oh, Christmas Tree,
How pleasant is thy fragrance?

THE BARD'S rich and pleasant voice filled the room, and Corin thoroughly enjoyed the lovely song, though he couldn't be sure whether it was anything like the songs Will remembered. Regardless, the melody sounded good to him, and it wasn't like they could ask Will beforehand whether or not they'd gotten it right.

"Well, what do you think?" Anri asked when the bard had finished.

They both looked at him expectantly.

"I think it sounds like a fun song. I'm sure Will's going to like it. It just reminded me that I need to go get the Christmas tree for the great hall still." He chuckled nervously and ran a hand through his hair. "And I need to figure out how to put lights on it too. Will said they had lights made of electricity on their Christmas trees, but I don't think yellow dragons can do anything like that without frying the branches off."

Nestar chuckled as he lowered his instrument. "I'm sure you'll figure something out, young rider. If there's nothing else for me to do here, I think I'll head back to the music hall to finish preparing for tonight's feast."

"Thank you, Bard Nestar," Anri said with a nod.

The bard gave a polite bow and stepped out.

Anri turned to Corin with an arched eyebrow, cradling Trouble in her arms. "You still don't have a plan for getting the tree?"

Corin blinked, bemused. "What do you mean? Why would I need a plan? I just have to go get it."

Anri shook her head in disappointment. "I swear, you yellow riders are as bad as the reds when it comes to thinking things through."

"What's that supposed to mean?" Corin folded his arms and scowled at her.

On the floor behind Anri, Jade lifted her head with a soft growl of irritation.

"You need to plan for things like this, Corin! Have you thought about it at all?" Anri held up her hand and one by one, ticked off her objections with her fingers.

"When do you plan to get the tree? How do you plan to cut it down? How do you plan to carry it? How do you plan to get it into the great hall without destroying it? And how do you plan to do all of that without Will seeing it, if you're so set on this party being a surprise?"

"I'm going to go get it tomorrow, for your information! What's up with you, anyway?" Corin snapped, his frustration boiling over. Here he was trying to do something nice for their friend, and all Anri could do was find problems with it.

Anri bristled at the tone of his voice, her hands on her hips and jaw clenched tight.

Trouble, sensing the tension between them, jumped onto Anri's shoulder with her fluffy striped tail bristling.

"What's with me? What do you mean?" Anri asked in a challenging tone.

Corin took a deep breath before finally letting out all his pent up frustration. "You've been snappy and dismissive about this whole party from the beginning. Everyone else is working together to make Christmas fun for Will. Why can't you just enjoy it like the rest of us? I thought you were supposed to be his friend!"

Anri's face froze in shock. On the floor by the door, Jade shrank down and gave a pained squawk before lashing her green tail restlessly.

"If you care about this party so much," Corin went on, "then maybe you could help me distract Will when I bring in the tree instead of criticizing everything I try to do. That's what a real friend would do."

Anri's breath caught. She dropped her hands to her sides and stepped back. To Corin's horror, tiny tears glistened in the corners of her eyes, and her chin trembled.

Instantly, his anger cooled and his face reddened with shame. "Swarms, Anri. I'm sorry. I—I went too far. I didn't mean—" Corin stammered, desperate to apologize.

"Don't say that," Anri interrupted, her voice low and trembling.

"What, swarms? Come on, you say it all the time!"

"No." She shook her head in irritation and looked away. "That you didn't mean it. You did mean it. You think I'm not a good friend. Well, maybe I'm not. But I try to be. To Will, Rin, and even to you." She lifted her face and met his gaze. Tears still glistened in her eyes, but they hadn't spilled over yet. She set her jaw firm and steadied her breathing before continuing. "And part of being a good friend is saying what needs to be said, even if it's not easy or fun."

Corin lowered his head, another wave of shame washing over him. He couldn't bring himself to meet

Anri's eyes as she turned and stomped away with Jade trotting after her.

"Well, now I've really messed up," he muttered to himself.

Leika padded over and nuzzled his hand until he started scratching her nose and ears.

Anri's mad, but she cares, Leika said. Her big green eyes shone up at him. *She wants to be your friend.*

"You're right," Corin sighed. "I need to make it up to her. Maybe I can talk to her after we get the Christmas tree tomorrow."

CHAPTER 6

Corin's breath clouded in the chilly air as he and Leika ambled through the icy foothills of Fire Mountain. The frosted grass crunched underfoot, its usually golden-green hue transformed into a shimmering carpet of white. Among the sloping, rocky terrain, the scattered pine trees stood tall, their needles coated in a thin layer of frost, giving them a silvery sheen.

"All right, Leika, that perfect tree we found must be around here somewhere. We should have marked it somehow. Do you remember which one it was?" Corin asked, resting the axe handle on his shoulder. His warm overcoat, lined with soft cormant down, shielded him from the worst of the cold, but the biting wind still stung his nose and ears, making him wish for the warm air of the dragonhold.

That morning, Rin had promised that she and the other young red riders would keep Will out of the way while he fetched the Christmas tree. They hadn't specified how they would do it, but knowing Rin, Corin assumed it had something to do with food.

Leika, unperturbed by the cold, took her time, her thick yellow hide reflecting the weak sunlight as she sniffed at various tree trunks. She snuffled her nose against the frosty ground and snorted. *This smells like the right place. I can smell your scent all over the ground where we picked up pinecones.*

"What? You can smell me?" Corin laughed.

Leika lifted her head and blinked, wiggling her ears in amusement. *Of course, I can. Especially when you forget to take a bath.*

"Now that's taking it too far," Corin warned with a grin, waggling a finger at her. "You're the one who'd leave the dirt on your hide until you're more brown than yellow."

But I'm also the one who can smell your scent on the ground here, she said, her ears tilted back smugly. Then she snaked her neck around and sniffed at the piles of dry orange pine needles. *It's this way.*

"Okay, then. Lead the way, Wonder-Nose."

Leika led him downhill to a clearing that Corin soon recognized as the place where they'd gathered the sack full of pinecones on their first trip to the foothills. Her nose snuffling and blowing, the yellow dragon finally stopped at the base of a bushy green pine tree. *Is this the right one?*

"Yeah, that's it!" Corin exclaimed, jogging in a quick circle around it. "Leika, you wonderful dragon. I'd never have found it without you!"

Leika gave a happy squawk and flapped her wings.

"Now I just have to hack it down, I guess." He hefted the axe. "All right, keep clear. Here it goes." He swung the axe around with all his might.

Thwack.

A chip of bark flaked off the trunk.

Thwack.

A sliver of white wood flew off.

Thwack.

A tiny piece broke away, several inches above where he'd aimed the blade of his axe.

Corin paused to examine the gouges in the wood. Thin cuts in the bark oozed thick, sticky sap. "Huh, this might take longer than I thought."

I know you can do it. Keep trying. Can I help? Leika

stepped forward, lifting her front claws as though to scratch the tree trunk with them.

"Better not." He waved her off. "I don't want to hit you with the blade by accident."

Leika stepped back again, and Corin lifted the axe determinedly. Then he resumed hacking.

Thwack. Thwack. Thwack. The sound of steel striking wood echoed through the forest, each blow ringing out with the same slow but determined pace. Corin swung the axe over and over, biting into the flesh of the tree inch by inch with his blade.

As he worked, the handle of the axe rubbed into his palms, first mildly irritating, then hot, and finally excruciatingly painful. Sweat dripped from his forehead in spite of the cold, soaking his tunic and making it cling to his skin under the coat. His arms and back ached with every swing, and his muscles trembled with exhaustion.

The gouge in the trunk grew wider and wider, and the tree shuddered and swayed with every strike, but it refused to fall.

Corin groaned and dropped the axe to the ground, wincing as he inspected the blisters forming on his hands.

"I don't think I can keep this up much longer,

Leika," he said, unbuttoning his coat to let some heat out and staring up at the towering pine. It loomed over him, proud and unyielding, like it was mocking him for his pathetic efforts at chopping it down.

Can I help now? Leika asked, dancing eagerly on her front feet.

"Well . . . okay, but you'll have to let me clean the sap off your claws later."

Leika sniffed dismissively, then focused on the trunk of the tree where the axe had gnawed it down. Her green eyes narrowed. She flared her wings, opened her mouth a little, then a bright bolt of electricity shot from her nose, striking the wood with a loud crack. The tree shuddered. The wood where the bolt struck popped and splintered, leaving a charred, broken gouge.

Corin sat up to look. "Hey, that's not a bad idea!"

Leika approached the uphill side of the tree, reared up on her hind legs, and leaned her weight into the branches. Though she was light for her size, the weakened trunk still gave a loud crack.

"That's brilliant, Leika. Let's finish it off together," Corin said, grabbing a low branch on the downhill side and pulling while Leika pushed with all her might. The mangled and scorched wood crackled and snapped, and the tree began to lean.

Corin realized just in time that he was on the wrong side of the tree. He jumped out of the way, branches scraping against his arms and side, just as the pine finally gave way, crashing to the ground with a rustling thud.

Corin and Leika exchanged triumphant grins, both panting with exhaustion.

"We did it!" Corin laughed and pumped his fist into the air.

Leika bugled in victory and leaped into the air, circling the fallen tree with a few strong flaps of her wings.

"Now that the hard part is over, all we have to do is get it back to the dragonhold!" Corin said, heaving a tired sigh.

He picked up the axe and slid the handle under his belt. Sticky pine sap covered his hands and clothes. He wondered how he would ever manage to clean it all off, but that was a problem for later.

"I guess I can just grab one of these thick lower branches and haul it on up," he said, putting actions to words. His blistered hands grasped a knobby lower branch, his arms shaking with weariness as he heaved the trunk over his shoulder.

The tree was heavier than he expected, digging into his neck and leaving sap stuck to his face. His weakened and sore fingers struggled to maintain their grip.

"Aw, stinging swarms!" he griped, trudging forward a single weary step. "Really?"

What's the matter? Leika asked.

"This stinging tree! It's so heavy!" Corin replied, trudging forward another step. Suddenly, the distance back to the dragonhold felt a lot farther than it had moments earlier.

I'll help! Leika offered, dropping to the ground and bounding over to him.

"Aw, Leika. You don't have to," Corin protested.

I want to. Really!

"Okay. Well, if you can grab another branch and help pull it up the hill. I think if we can get over that steep ledge up ahead, it'll be easier. The ground is more level after that."

Leika clutched a branch between her teeth and crawled backward, tugging the tree along with Corin. Bit by bit, they moved it uphill, leaving a trail of scraped dirt and pine needles behind them.

As they neared the ledge, Corin could tell that Leika was growing weary. Her breathing was coming quicker, and she needed to rest longer between each tug.

"Are you doing okay, girl?" Corin panted.

My jaw is tired. And this tree tastes awful!

"I bet it does. Do you want to take a break?" he asked.

Leika gave her branch an extra hard tug, dragging the tree up against the steep ledge. *I want to help. I'll get this tree on top of the ledge for you. I can do it.*

"All right, if you're sure. Hold it steady for me while I climb up to the top. Then we can pull it up together."

Leika did as he said, and when he crouched at the top of the ledge, clutching the trunk, she jumped up next to him and resumed her grip on the branch.

"Let's get it up here. Ready? Pull!" Corin shouted.

Leika pulled, and Corin heaved. Leika's claws strained and slipped in the icy grass while the blisters on Corin's palms flared with pain. His arms felt like pudding.

Then the trunk slipped out of his hands.

As the tree dropped, the branch in Leika's mouth snapped, leaving her with a broken stick clutched between her teeth. The tree thumped against the corner of the ledge and bounced back.

"Oh, no!" Corin shouted, reaching out to catch it. But it was too late. The tree bounced out of reach and rolled back, gaining speed as it fell down the hill. It crashed into a boulder, bounced to the side, and tumbled all the way down the hill, smashing into tree trunks along the way before finally coming to rest among a cluster of dark thorny bushes at the bottom of the hill.

Corin stared at the disaster in numb shock. Guilt and shame started swirling through his mind until he realized they weren't his own feelings but Leika's, filtering to him through the connection they shared.

I'm sorry, she said. *I couldn't lift the tree for you. I tried.*

"No, don't feel bad about that," Corin said, patting her head until he realized he was smearing sap on her horns. He wiped his palm against his tunic, then gently removed the broken branch from her jaws. "It's not your fault. You did great. This tree is just a lot heavier than I thought it would be. It's my fault, really."

Leika gave a soft croon and leaned her head into his side.

Corin took a deep breath and let out a resigned sigh. "How about we go take a look? Maybe it's not too bad."

Thoroughly exhausted and stumbling with weariness, Corin made his way down the hill. Leika took to the air, staying close overhead, flying in tight circles as she followed him to where the ill-fated tree had landed.

As Corin drew near, he groaned in dismay and flopped to the ground, resting his arms on his knees and hanging his head.

Jagged wooden spikes protruded from the tree where branches ought to have been. Other branches were nearly bare of needles. The top of the tree had snapped clean off.

Is it bad? Leika asked.

"It's ruined," Corin answered, voice heavy. "There's no way we can use this tree now."

CHAPTER 7

Corin slumped in defeat, gazing at the ruin that was once their perfect Christmas tree. Exhaustion weighed on him, and he felt like giving up. How would they get another tree in time for Christmas? He was too drained to chop down another one, let alone haul it back to the dragonhold. And with tomorrow being Christmas Day, they had no chance of finding a new tree in time.

"I should have listened to Anri. Stinging swarms! That girl is annoying, but she was right. I should have had a plan for how to do this."

Leika let out a curious little chirp and then landed in the clearing uphill from him.

Anri doesn't like to play or have fun very much, but she does like to think before doing things, she said.

"I've noticed," Corin replied wryly.

Leika paused for a moment and then continued, *She notices things too.*

Confused, Corin lifted his head to look at Leika.

A bright spark lit up in Leika's eye, and she swished her tail excitedly.

"What are you talking about? What does she notice?"

She notices that we need help. Leika pointed her nose up the hill. A small green dragon circled in the air, followed by a huge red dragon high overhead. Then a figure appeared on the crest of the hill, silhouetted against the sky's fading light. It was Anri, peering down at them.

"Tumi, I've found them!" Anri shouted. "Down here!"

"Anri!?" Corin exclaimed, laughing in disbelief mixed with relief. "What are you doing here?"

Anri jogged down the hill, her kisnit bounding after her in the frosty grass. "I saw you leave the dragonhold with no way to carry a tree back and only a wood-splitting hatchet to chop it down with, so I figured you might need some help," she said with a wry half-smile.

Corin let out a relieved chuckle and raked his hands through his hair, wincing as the sticky sap clung to his blistered palms. "Yeah, we kind of do."

The huge red dragon overhead circled and tipped her nose down to eye them. Corin recognized her as Ruby, the dragon belonging to their flapling instructor, Tumi.

As Tumi himself appeared at the top of the hill, dark and broad-shouldered, he flashed a friendly smile and jogged down to their level.

"Hello, Corin. It looks like we got here just in time. How about we cut down a nice tree for the great hall, hm?" Tumi wielded a handheld saw with a grin.

Corin sighed with relief and nodded gratefully. "Yeah, that would be perfect. Thank you, Tumi!"

With Tumi's help, they found a tree that was easily twice as tall as the one Corin had attempted to chop down. Corin wasn't even sure whether it would fit in the great hall, but Tumi assured him it would look festive in the corner next to the fire pit where the ceiling was highest.

The sharp-toothed saw sliced through the thick trunk with a few minutes of work, and the new tree crashed to the ground with a flourish of bouncing branches and a spray of frosted pine needles.

With the tree felled, Ruby landed in the clearing, and they managed to tie it to her back between her wings. The huge red dragon easily hauled it up the hill with her rider while Corin walked alongside Anri, who carried her kisnit in her arms and absently scratched the soft fur of her cheeks. Leika and Jade followed after them, chirping happily to one another.

"Hey, Anri," Corin began, breaking the silence between them.

She looked up at him, her expression unreadable.

"I'm really sorry about what I said yesterday," Corin said, his voice softening.

Her eyes dropped to the ground, and he could sense the hurt he had caused radiating through her silence.

"I wasn't thinking," he continued. "That's something I have a problem with. I always seem to do and say things without thinking them through."

Anri sighed. "And I always speak before I consider how my words might affect others," she replied, meeting his gaze and offering a small smile and shrug.

Corin offered a crooked smile in return. "Thanks for coming to my rescue today," he said.

Anri snorted and rolled her eyes. "You hardly needed rescuing. But I knew how much getting a Christmas tree for Will meant to you, and I didn't want you to be disappointed."

"Now that we have one, everything will be perfect tomorrow!" Corin exclaimed with a grin.

Anri chuckled and shook her head slightly.

"What? You don't think so?"

"I hope so, for your sake and Will's. Let's just leave it at that."

With a nod they continued following the huge red dragon and their new Christmas tree back towards the dragonhold.

THE GREAT HALL, an expansive room carved directly from the mountain, stood still in the quiet of early morning. Pale light glinted through the colored glass high in the ceiling, hinting at the beauty that would come alive when the sun rose. The rows of stone tables were empty for now, but the great hall was soon buzzing with excitement as young dragon riders, some still bleary-eyed from sleep, streamed in, eager to prepare for the grand celebration they'd been planning for weeks.

The new tree fit snugly in the corner by the hearth, just as Tumi had predicted, and with the help of Anri and Corin, they had hammered cross beams into the trunk to ensure it stood upright. Even before a single ornament had been hung, the tree emanated a sense of merry festivity that enveloped the room.

"This is wonderful!" Corin exclaimed, beaming with pride as he surveyed the room. Many of the younger kids were still rubbing their eyes and stifling yawns, having woken up extra early to make sure everything was ready before Will arrived. "I think I want to have a Christmas tree every year from now on."

Rin nodded in agreement, eyeing the massive tree skeptically. "It looks so heavy, though," she said. "How'd you get it here?"

Corin brushed the question off with a dismissive wave of his hand. "Oh, it was hardly any trouble at all."

Anri shot him an amused look. "Tumi and Ruby helped him," she told Rin.

Corin chuckled. "It was Anri, really. I wouldn't have asked for their help if it hadn't been for her."

Anri's wry smile shifted to one of surprise.

"Merry Christmas, everyone! Let's get it all set up before Will gets here," Tumi exclaimed, clapping his hands together to rally the group.

The room erupted in a chorus of "Merry Christmas," and the young flapling riders scurried off to set up the party.

CHAPTER 8

With everyone working together, the great hall bustled with eager festive activity.

Beck and the other members of the blue wing carefully placed crystalline ice sculptures, crafted by their dragons, in the center of the banquet tables.

The yellow wing busied themselves with handmade decorations, placing little wooden reindeer and Father Christmas figures with white beards and red coats.

Meanwhile the red wing made their way to the kitchen and began emerging with platters of delicious treats, including sweet biscuits coated in white sugar and shaped like snowflakes and bells, a platter of succulent roasted cormant meat, and bowls of punch, accompanied by red and white candy shaped like curved canes.

Corin began work on the tree itself, carefully hanging his yellow-painted pinecones on the branches. After the thick paint had dried, the overpowering smell had all but vanished, leaving behind a faint hint of sulfur. Still, the resulting finish was less than satisfactory. The yellow paint was powdery and tended to flake off at the slightest touch.

But Corin wasn't too concerned. He knew the ornaments only had to last for the morning surprise party, and that was all that mattered. Despite that, he couldn't shake the feeling that something was missing—a finishing touch that would make the tree truly spectacular.

As he pondered this, Rin's voice interrupted his thoughts. He turned to see her holding a big bowl of milky, frothy liquid and calling out to him.

"Hey, Corin! Did Will tell you anything about eggnog? What it's supposed to smell or taste like, I mean?"

"Eggnog?" Corin furrowed his brow, struggling to remember whether Will had said anything about it. "I don't know. Why do you ask?"

"I found an off-lander recipe for it. It's supposed to be traditional for Christmas. But I couldn't read the recipe very well. Do you think it's supposed to have chunks of soft cheese in it?"

Corin's nose wrinkled in disgust. Who would put cheese in a drink? "That sounds really gross."

"I know, but they also have this thing called cheese-cake, so I thought it might be right. It sort of smells like cheese too."

"Is this the one you were talking about that has a lot of firedew in it?"

Rin nodded.

Corin gave a nonchalant shrug. "As long as you followed the recipe as closely as you could, I think it will be fine."

Rin nodded again, satisfied, and carefully placed her bowl of creamy curdled punch on the tabletop.

Then Beck and the other blue riders approached him. "Our dragons are waking up now. Should we position them around the balcony to prepare to make snow?" Beck asked.

"Um . . . yeah. If they don't mind waiting there until Will arrives. By the way, do any of you have ideas on how to put lights on the tree?"

"What kind of lights? Like lanterns?" Jayda asked.

"Will said that in the off-lands, they have lights made of electricity," Corin explained. "But I don't think we can do that, can we?"

The blue riders shook their heads in unison.

"I think the tree looks nice as it is," Liza said. "It's a pity you only found yellow paint, though. Some red would look great with the green and yellow."

"Red, huh?" Corin scrutinized the tree. The bright-yellow pinecones shone like beacons among the dark-green branches. But Liza was right; adding some red color would make it look more festive.

Frowning in thought, Corin rubbed his chin and furrowed his brow. What could he use to add some red to the tree? How could he put lights on the branches? Red decorations and small lights . . . Red . . . lights . . .

Just like that, the answer flashed in his mind. He snapped his fingers and grinned. "I've got it! The candles!"

Corin darted out of the great hall, past curious stares from the other kids, and into the courtyard. The eastern sky behind Smoketree Peak glowed pale blue, heralding the coming sunrise. He was running out of time.

Most of the young dragons were still slumbering in a cozy pile on the smooth, warm volcanic rock outside the barracks. As Corin ran by, Leika lifted her head from Ember's back and blinked sleepily at him. *Where are you going?*

"I'm going to get that box of red candles from the

storage room," he said. "They'll be perfect for the Christmas tree!"

Leika slowly stretched and yawned while Corin made his way into the dim storage room. He had visited the place enough times by now that he didn't have to search among the boxes to locate the candlesticks. He knew exactly where they were. But he did need to leave the door open for light to find a spool of thin wire and sturdy clippers. Those would be perfect for attaching the candles to the branches.

As he made his way back through the courtyard, Leika was just finishing her morning stretches. She spotted him and bounded over, flapping her wings a few times to glide over the ground and reach him faster.

You found lights to put on the tree? she asked.

"That's right. I don't know why I didn't think of it sooner. Candles! I'll just twist some wire around them to keep them on, and they'll be perfect. The red will look nice against the green branches too."

Fun! I want to see!

"Sure you can! The blues are already in there getting ready to make snow."

Leika hopped along happily after him until they reached the entrance.

As Corin stepped into the great hall, for a moment he was awestruck. With the room now decked out for the celebration, it had transformed from the cool and majestic space he was used to. The stained glass windows sparkled in the radiance of the rising sun, casting brilliant hues over tables now piled high with a festive feast.

The brass chandeliers, with their flickering candles, made the entire hall glow with a warm golden light.

He could see the kids from the blue wing already heading up to the balcony with their dragons, eager to have them begin showering the whole room with snow.

And the food! Corin's eyes darted from one mouthwatering dish to another. Among the piles of familiar foods, he spotted unfamiliar treats from the off-lands: cookies that looked like tiny people, curved sticks of hard candy with red stripes, snowflake-shaped biscuits dusted in white sugar, and the thick milky drink Rin had been raving about. What had she called it? Eggnog?

To one side, the massive hearth roared, large enough to hold a whole tree trunk. Beside it, young riders from the yellow wing hung red woolen stockings in preparation for the festivities.

Bard Nestar had taken up his position on the platform at the head of the room, strumming an unfamiliar but festive-sounding tune on his mandolin. And in a prominent corner by the hearth, the massive pine tree with Corin's yellow-painted pinecones towered over everything.

"Oh, this is so awesome!" Corin breathed. "I can't wait for Will to see this!"

He hurried over to the fireplace to collect some of the long matches and began cutting lengths of wire for the candles. As he started twisting the wires around the branches, others showed up to help. Anri took the clippers and started cutting the wires. Some of the kids from the yellow wing started twisting the wires around the candles and piling them up. Rin and the others gathered around to collect the prepared candles and fasten them to the boughs of the tree.

As the last of the candles was being fixed into place, Corin took a match and started lighting them. The others joined in as well. One by one, the waxed wicks flickered to life, giving off a warm, welcoming glow.

As they worked, more people started entering the great hall. Older dragon riders, healers, herdsmen, archivists—all murmuring in admiration as they made their way to the tables.

Corin and his friends had to use up a few of the long hearth matches before the job was done, and they had to stand on ladders to reach the uppermost candles. But when the last flame was lit, everyone stepped back to admire the tree.

"Wow!" Corin breathed.

It is very beautiful! Leika said, gazing at the tree in awe as she sat in the aisle by the door.

He turned to flash her a smile and saw the light of a hundred candles dancing in his dragon's eyes.

The yellow-painted pinecones peeked out like bright stars among the shadows of the massive tree. The flickering flames of the red candles nestled between the branches cast a warm glow throughout the room. The area around the tree was filled with the sweet scent of pine, and Corin couldn't help but be mesmerized by the sheer beauty of it all.

Rin stepped forward, hand outstretched as if she couldn't believe what she was seeing. "It's so beautiful," she whispered, eyes wide with wonder.

Beck nodded in agreement, his mouth slightly agape as he took in the sight. "I'd heard stories of Christmas trees before, but I never imagined they would be like this."

The group slowly made their way around the tree, admiring its beauty from every angle. Watching as the flickering flames cast dancing shadows on the bright yellow ornaments.

"My, this really is something!" Dragonlord Brom's voice boomed merrily across the great hall.

They all turned, and the crowded hall burst into

joyful laughter when everyone saw their large imposing dragonlord dressed in a long red robe lined with thick brown fur and wearing a comical bright-red cap.

"Merry Christmas, young dragon riders," Brom announced, holding out a heavy sack loaded with presents. He let out a deep merry laugh. "You've done a splendid job decorating the great hall. I love what you've accomplished here!"

"I think it's time to start the party. I'll go get Will!" Corin offered.

"That's right, we can't start this off-lander Christmas party without him!" Brom said with a chuckle. Then he paused and sniffed the air. "Does it smell like sulphurix in here to anyone else?"

Corin was already on his way to the door, but as he left, he heard Rin say, "I thought so too. But maybe it's just the eggnog. It has cooked egg in it and smells kind of . . . smelly."

CHAPTER 9

As Corin made his way back to the barracks to fetch Will, he passed by some of the dragonhold residents who were crossing the courtyard. The warm volcanic air carried their voices as they greeted him in festive red, black, and yellow garbs. Their smiles were bright, and some held small gifts wrapped in colorful fabric and tied with green ribbons. Walking arm in arm toward the great hall, they broke into snippets of familiar Christmas songs, filling the air with the joyful spirit of the season.

Leika took to the air and followed Corin from above, circling him in excited twirls and swoops. *This is fun. Everyone is so happy. Is Christmas always like this?* she asked.

"It should be," Corin replied. "What's the point if

you're not having fun, right?" He paused and rubbed his chin in thought, grimacing slightly as the motion rubbed a painful blister on his palm. "But what about Will? How does he feel? Is he excited about Christmas? Can you tell?"

Leika landed and trotted alongside him, folding her leathery wings. She cocked her head and blinked silently for a moment. *Vortex says he's already awake. He feels happy to me. Or . . . at least not sad. Sleepy still. We all went to bed late last night after the Christmas Eve bonfire.*

Corin snorted a laugh. "Yeah, but this is Christmas morning! Who wouldn't wake up early for that? Let's go get them!"

When they made it into the barracks, Corin and Leika found Will still getting ready for the day. The young dragon rider was tying his belt around his tunic, his hair in disarray from sleep.

Vortex lay nearby on his sleeping mat, his brilliant hide visible even in the shadows. His pale form was ghostly white against the volcanic rock walls, his amber eyes shining at them. As they entered, he opened his mouth in a huge toothy yawn.

"Hey, Corin. Hi, Leika. Merry Christmas," Will said, running his hand through his messy hair. "You two were up early." He yawned and stretched, his back popping in protest. "Normally I'm the one who has to drag you out of bed for training."

Corin laughed. "We aren't training today! It's Christmas in Fire Mountain Dragonhold! Aren't you excited?"

Will sat on the edge of his cot and started tugging on his boots. "Well, yeah, I guess. I mean, we've been having Christmas parties every day for the last few weeks. Like Anri said before, it kind of gets old after a while." He shrugged.

"But today is different. It's Christmas morning! Come on—I bet you'll like the party. Let's go!" Corin bounced on his toes, eager to get started.

Will exchanged a glance with Vortex, the two of them silently communicating. Corin could sense Will's hesitation. Was he really that disappointed with Christmas in Avria? Corin decided he had to convince Will to be excited for the party somehow!

"Please, Will. I promise you'll like this party. It's going to be so much more amazing than all the others. You'll see. Everyone's going to remember this Christmas party for their whole lives."

Finally, Will gave a crooked smile, shrugged, and nodded. "Okay, yeah. Let's go. It is Christmas, after all."

"Yes!" Corin exclaimed, jumping and pumping his

arm. "I can't wait for you to see what this party is going to be like. I promise you won't regret it."

As they hurried across the courtyard, Corin asked Leika to let the blue dragons know they were on their way, signaling the start of the surprise.

It's time to make it snow in the great hall, he told her, grinning mischievously.

A moment later, Leika reported back. *Icicle says they've started. Tundra says it's fun to make frost breath inside, even if it's not as easy in the warm air,* she said, relaying the message from the blue dragons.

Corin laughed, imagining the blue dragons spraying snow and ice around the great hall in delight.

"What's so funny?" Will asked.

"Never mind," Corin said, shaking his head and stifling a chuckle. "I'll tell you later. Here we are." He pulled Will through the main doors of the dragonhold, bouncing on the balls of his feet and unable to keep the grin off his face.

As they entered the anteroom outside the great hall, Anri greeted them with Trouble perched on her shoulder, the kisnit twitching her huge pointy ears. "Everything is ready," she announced, nodding at Corin.

Will looked at Corin suspiciously. "Ready? What do you mean? What are you guys up to?"

Anri shook her head and pursed her lips. "It's all Corin and Rin's doing. Don't blame me for any of this."

"Wait a minute. You helped out a lot," Corin interjected, pointing a finger at Anri. "You have to take some of the credit."

Will frowned and looked back and forth between the two of them. "All right, wait a minute. You two were working together? Now I'm really curious."

Anri motioned towards the ornate iron doors that led to the great hall. "Go in and see," she said with a sly grin.

Together they pushed the doors open and were instantly transported into a magical winter wonderland.

Will's eyes widened as he took in the enchanting scene before them. The young blue dragons perched in the high corners of the balcony, taking turns breathing frost into the air that crystallized and cascaded down in flurries of chilling snow. Although the snow melted instantly when it touched the warm stone floor, it was still a breathtaking sight.

The dripping ice centerpieces on the tables glistened with refracted color and light, perfectly complementing the festive food and bright decorations.

As they walked into the great hall, Nestar's merry tune filled the air. His mandolin strummed with an upbeat melody that echoed throughout the room, adding to the festive atmosphere.

Dragonlord Brom, sitting at the head table, called out, "Merry Christmas!" Wearing his fur-lined red robe, he looked remarkably like Father Christmas.

Will's eyes widened when he saw the towering Christmas tree dominating the corner of the room. Adorned with shining red candles and bright-yellow pinecone decorations, it was a beautiful sight.

"Is that a Christmas tree? Really? How?" he asked.

Corin laughed and held up his blistered palms. "Well, I can tell you it wasn't easy. But it was definitely worth it. Now I want to have a Christmas tree every year!"

Will's attention was then diverted by Rin, who ran up to them with a mug of thick, creamy, yellow liquid. "Here, Will. We made this especially for you. It's eggnog! I hope we got it right," she said, thrusting the sloshing mug into his hands.

Will took it with a bemused smile and sipped the eggnog. Corin noticed a flash of disgust on his friend's face as he pulled the mug away from his lips. Will quickly adjusted his features and swallowed the mouthful as they followed Rin to one of the tables.

"Thanks," he said, hastily placing the mug on the table, a little farther away than strictly necessary. "Did you guys really do all of this for me? The snow, the eggnog, the gingerbread men, and candy canes? The songs? The Christmas tree?"

"Of course, we did," Rin said with a warm smile. "We're your friends."

"Yeah," Corin added. "We wanted you to have a fun Christmas with the rest of us."

"Wow, I can't believe it!" Will blinked as his eyes traveled around the room again.

Corin was about to say something in response, but his attention was drawn by an ominous sizzling sound coming from the direction of the Christmas tree.

He turned his head just in time to see a shower of sparks erupting from one of the yellow-painted pinecones where the flame of a candle was touching it.

Before Corin could react, the pinecone exploded with a deafening pop, sending a shower of blue and red sparkles cascading down the side of the tree. The crackling sound of burning wood filled the air as flames licked at the surrounding branches.

In an instant, more yellow cones erupted into sprays of blue sparks and balls of fire, and the tree was engulfed in a wall of bright-orange flames. The intense heat and blinding light pulsed through the corner of the dining hall, causing Corin's skin to tingle and his eyes to water.

People started screaming and shouting, pushing back their chairs and jumping away from their tables to get away from the inferno.

Dragonlord Brom's booming voice broke through the chaos: "Flapling riders, get back! Out of the dining hall! Red riders, get the children away and douse the fire!"

The scorching heat made it hard for Corin to breathe as he scrambled to his feet, his boots slipping on the wet floor. The pungent scent of burning pine needles mixed with the acrid odor of smoke filled his nostrils. He stumbled and landed in a slushy puddle formed by the snow and melting ice formations on the tables.

Rin grabbed his arm and helped him up, her face etched with panic. "Corin! Are you alright?"

"The—the tree!" he stammered. "What happened? It exploded! I can't believe it!" His mind raced but went nowhere. All he could think was that everything was ruined and somehow it must be his fault.

"Will, Anri, get him out of here. I'm going to help with the fire," Rin said.

"No! You'll get hurt," he protested, still reeling in shock.

"Don't be silly, Corin." She flashed him a quick smile. "Red riders can't get burned, remember? I'll be fine."

He watched as she ran towards the fire, her red tunic standing out in the chaos. She was right, of course. What was he thinking?

The room echoed with shouts and screams and the roar of the fire as the young dragon riders scrambled towards the exit away from the tree, which was now nothing more than a tower of flames. Thick black smoke billowed across the ceiling, filling the room and making it hard to see.

The red dragon riders sprang into action, their faces set in determined grimaces as they beat the flames with damp cloths and cast buckets of water at the inferno. Their goal was obvious: contain the fire and prevent it from spreading any further.

Fearless of the fire, some of the riders dove headfirst into the flames, impervious to the intense heat and grabbing burning branches with their bare hands. They twisted and snapped the fiery wood, smothering the flames and stopping them in their tracks.

Meanwhile, Will and Anri guided Corin through the chaos, their grip on his arms firm. Corin's eyes remained fixed on the burning tree, his heart pounding in his chest as he watched it sway and creak like a living thing fighting against its own destruction.

And then, with a deafening crack, the tree toppled over. It crashed down onto the tables, sending a shower of sparks and embers raining down on the surrounding area. The flames leaped and danced, engulfing everything in their path: the Christmas stockings, the wreaths, the garlands. The ice formations shattered into a million pieces, sending sharp shards flying through the air.

Corin's throat burned with the choking smoke, and he coughed and gagged as he stumbled along in Will and Anri's grasp. But even as he fled from the danger, his mind was filled with a single, haunting image: the burning tree, a once-beautiful symbol of the holiday season, now reduced to nothing more than a smoldering ruin.

CHAPTER 10

orin, Will, and Anri stood in the courtyard alongside the other non-red riders and residents of the dragonhold. The air was thick with smoke and the sharp smell of burned pine, a stark contrast to the festive atmosphere of moments before.

Through the haze billowing from the open door, Master Healer Uther moved with purpose. The short, elderly man with neat white hair wore his traditional white and blue healer's robes. His kind face, always observant, looked for signs of distress among the crowd. His soft yet clear voice offered instructions and comfort as his gentle hands checked for injuries, applying soothing salve where needed. Thankfully, nobody seemed to have been seriously hurt.

Breaking the heavy silence, Will's voice was low and concerned: "You okay, Corin?"

Anri furrowed her brow, looking at him with a mix of worry and sympathy. "I think he might be in shock."

Corin remained silent, his mind still reeling from the chaos that had just unfolded.

Leika, sensing his distress, swooped down from her perch and nuzzled him gently. Without thinking, Corin's hand found its way to her soft yellow ears and stubby horns. He took a deep breath and blinked slowly.

"I don't know what happened," he mumbled. "We worked so hard to make it the perfect Christmas . . . How could it go so wrong?" As Corin spoke his voice trembled with confusion and regret.

Tumi, the flapling trainer, emerged from the main doors, holding a yellow and black lump in his hand. "We've found the problem. Someone painted these pinecones with sulphurix."

Corin's heart sank at his words. "Sulphurix? I've never even heard of that."

"It's a pyrotechnic powder we use for training red dragons," Tumi explained. "When a dragon flames a target loaded with a bag of this, they get rewarded with a pretty display of blue sparks." Tumi raised his eyebrows at Corin. "You didn't know?"

Corin's knees nearly buckled. "I thought . . . So it wasn't yellow paint after all?"

Leika leaned into his side, offering him comfort and support.

Tumi shook his head. "No, I'm afraid not. Thankfully, no one was badly hurt, and now we just need to clean up the mess."

"I'm so sorry," Corin said, his voice choked and small.

"I know you didn't mean to cause any harm," Tumi replied kindly. "And thankfully, not too much harm was done. Nobody was seriously injured, and most of Fire Mountain Dragonhold is fireproof, for obvious reasons. You aren't the first flapping rider who started an accidental fire here. And I'm pretty sure you won't make the same mistake twice."

"N-no! Of course not!" Corin stammered.

Tumi gave a small chuckle. "That's what I thought. Now, let's get this mess cleaned up. Everyone needs to help, flapling riders included."

As Corin, Will, and Anri made their way back into the great hall with the others, they were struck by the stark contrast from what they had left only moments ago. In the aftermath of the fire, the dragonhold's great hall was unrecognizable. The lively and festive

Christmas wonderland had transformed into a desolate wasteland of slush, mud, and broken debris.

The once magnificent tree, which had stood tall and proud only moments before, was now a pathetic heap of charred and blackened branches. Its lifeless form lay scattered across the room, a stark reminder of the chaos that had erupted.

The food that had been so carefully prepared and displayed was now a ruined mess, contaminated by ash and mud, scattered carelessly on the ground. The garlands and wreaths that had once adorned the walls and ceiling were nothing more than ashes and charred fragments trampled underfoot.

The air was thick with the stench of scorched food and burned pine, mingled with the sour smell of Rin's eggnog that had been spilled in a desperate attempt to extinguish the flames.

Rin and the other red riders were already hard at work, covered in ash and working to pile up the charred remains of the tree in the corner of the hall. Rin straightened from her work, wiping her face, smudging it with black soot, and gave them a friendly wave.

"We're going to pile up the wood by the fireplace and burn it all off," Rin said. "That'll be easier than trying to haul it outside. And the kitchen staff is going to bring in crates for all the dishes and food. With everyone working together, it shouldn't take too long to clean everything up."

Corin sighed in resignation. He had been looking forward to a festive Christmas celebration, but now, cleaning up the great hall was the last thing he wanted to do. Even worse, he knew Will must be disappointed as well. Instead of creating a memorable experience for his friend, he had created a disaster that didn't feel like Christmas at all.

"It's too bad the eggnog is all gone," Rin said, frowning in apology at Will. "You barely got to taste it. Maybe I can make some more later."

Will quickly stifled a laugh before nodding with a more solemn expression. "It's okay, Rin," he said. "I appreciate it. But eggnog was never one of my favorite parts of Christmas, anyway."

For the next few hours, dragon riders and non-riders alike worked tirelessly to restore the great hall to its former glory. They piled up the charred remains of the once-magnificent tree and gathered the ruined feast into crates, while others washed the tables and scrubbed the soot-covered floor with soapy water and long-handled brushes. Corin worked hard through the lingering pain in the palms of his hands, determined to make amends for the disaster he had caused.

As they poured fresh buckets of soapy water over

the floor and scrubbed the soot-covered stones, Corin thought he heard a sob. He turned to see Will scrubbing the floor with shaking shoulders. For a moment Corin thought his friend was crying, and a fresh wave of guilt washed over him. Then Will turned around, and he saw that instead a bright smile was plastered on his friend's face.

Will was laughing.

"What?" Corin asked, stepping closer. He couldn't help but smile too, even though he didn't get what the joke was. "What's so funny?"

Curious, Rin and Anri came over to see what was going on.

"You guys really did all of this for me?" Will asked, another laugh escaping as he spoke. "But why?"

Rin answered first: "We noticed you weren't enjoying the Christmas celebrations as much as everyone else."

"I thought you'd have more fun if our Christmas was how you remembered it from the off-lands," Corin said.

"You are our friend, after all," Anri added.

Will laughed even louder and wiped tears from his eyes with the back of his hand. "I just can't believe it! Nobody's ever done anything like this for me before.

You really dragged a gigantic pine tree out of the forest to make a Christmas tree for me? Dragonlord Brom dressed up to look like Santa Claus? You even convinced the blue flaplings to make it snow! All because you thought I wasn't having enough fun?"

They all nodded, and Corin still felt ashamed that nothing had turned out the way he had planned. But Will laughed again and threw his arm around Corin's shoulder in an enthusiastic side hug. "You guys are the best! Thank you. You're the best friends anyone could have. I'll never forget this Christmas. Not ever!"

After they had cleared the ruined Christmas feast out of the great hall, and everyone had a chance to freshen up, the dragon riders continued their Christmas celebrations in the courtyard.

The young dragons pranced around, wearing reindeer antlers made by the yellow riders from tree branches. While Ember, Leika, and Vortex sported their antlers with pride, Jade flatly refused hers. The dragon riders donned crowns made of holly and red berries, and the bard played off-lander Christmas songs—with Will helping everyone to sing the right words.

Laughter and merriment filled the courtyard as the dragon riders celebrated an outdoor Christmas. The aroma of hot kaffa and spices mixed with the smoky scent of the bonfire as the red riders gathered around the towering flames with their dragons adding their fiery breath to the blaze. They shared sweet bread glistening with sugar and bowls of steaming hot Christmas punch.

As the day turned to night, warm and clear with twinkling stars above like distant diamonds, the air grew cool, and it was time to exchange Christmas gifts. Anri gave Will a handmade bow and arrow set, while Rin received a small knife, crafted by Anri's brother. Anri gave Corin a wooden staff, with a promise that she'd teach him how to use it properly. Rin gifted her friends little bags of hard candy—a recipe she had discovered while searching for off-lander Christmas dishes.

Will seemed a little shy as he handed out his hand-carved wooden dragons, each resembling their own dragons.

"They're amazing, Will!" Rin exclaimed, cradling the little wooden Ember in her palms. She held the figurine up for her dragon to see. "Ember, look—it's you!"

It surprised Corin to find that the little wooden dragon Will gave him looked remarkably like Leika. The playful expression on the tiny wooden face was perfect. "This is amazing. How did you make these, Will?"

"I bought the wood carving kit from the merchant

that visited us," Will answered with a casual shrug. "He was happy to take my old pair of boots for it."

Corin tucked the little dragon into his belt pouch and looked around at his friends. "I'm sorry, guys," he said, his face flushing in embarrassment. "With everything that was going on, I forgot to make any gifts."

"Are you kidding?" Will chuckled, giving Corin a playful punch on the shoulder. "I think you gave us the best present. We'll remember this Christmas forever because of you."

"Absolutely," Rin agreed, beaming. "We'll be telling the story of the incredible flaming Christmas tree to each other every year!"

Anri rolled her eyes, but her smirk betrayed her amusement. "I know I won't forget it—that's for sure."

Corin laughed with relief with his friends and ran his fingers through his hair. Rin passed around fresh hot mugs of creamy kaffa, and the bard struck up another festive Christmas tune. As they sat around the roaring bonfire, enveloped in the warmth and love of their friends and dragons, Corin knew this Christmas would indeed be one to remember.

IF YOU ENJOYED A Dragonhold Christmas, please consider leaving a review. Book reviews help readers find books they love, and fill authors' lives with joy!

DIVE into the pages ahead for a sneak peek of *Anri and the Dragon Quest*. Discover the captivating tale of how Anri discovered her dragon egg and embarked on her journey as a dragon rider of Avria.

N. A. DAVENPORT

ANRI *and the* DRAGON QUEST

DRAGON RIDERS OF AVRIA

Anri and the Dragon Quest

The door opened with a soft creak, letting a beam of golden light pierce the dim family room. Anri closed it quietly behind her as she stepped out, careful not to wake her little brother who was snoring softly on a pile of wool blankets in the corner.

Jaze would be hungry when he woke, Anri knew, but all they had left to eat was half a pot of cold, watery porridge. The coins tucked in the inner pocket of Anri's bag clinked together as she walked, money enough to get a piece of fish, perhaps, or maybe a small bag of kaffa seeds, but not enough to fill her family's bellies.

Anri frowned and hugged herself against the early morning chill. Dew clung to the tall stalks of grass and dandelion fluff, sparkling faintly in the pale light.

Heavy clanking echoed toward her from the shop up the hill. Her older brother, Jamero, was working metal already, and probably waking up some of their neighbors. Anri shook her head in amusement and turned to see what he was up to. As she neared the open door of the shop, Jamero looked up, his face red from the heat, sweat beading on his forehead.

"Getting an early start today?" she asked, cocking a half-smile.

He chuckled wearily. "I need to get these hames ready. I was supposed to have them done yesterday, but I just can't seem to get them to match the way Father used to." He lowered his eyes to the metal band he'd been beating into submission on the anvil.

Anri bit her lip. Their father had been a skilled master smith, the best in Silverlake. Jamero had become his apprentice as soon as he was old enough to wield a hammer, but he hadn't had time to master his skills before their father died from a sudden sickness a few years ago.

Some of their customers voiced their disappointment in the lower quality work. Others simply took their business elsewhere. With every customer that never came back, their family's situation became more desperate, until first their mother, and then Anri, was forced to take jobs to help.

"What are hames, anyway?" she asked, trying to change the subject.

Jamero wiped the dusty sweat from his forehead with a rag and held up the curved metal bar with a pair of tongs. Then he took another from the nearby bench, holding them side by side for her to see. They looked like mirror images to her eyes, except the finished one in his bare hand was smoother and had metal rings attached.

"They're part of a cormant harness," he said. "They go over their shoulders to carry the weight of the cart. See the loops here?" He pointed to metal rings on the finished one. "That's where the tracers attach."

She folded her arms and raised an eyebrow. "And tracers are . . ."

He laughed. "The ropes that attach them to the cart. Honestly, you see cormant carts every day, and you don't know these things?"

She snorted. "I don't work on them like you do."

Jamero shook his head with a half-grin. "Speaking of which, I'd better finish this soon or . . ." He didn't finish that thought. Instead, he turned away as though to examine his work in a better light.

Anri had never been good at giving moral support. She cast around in her mind, trying to find something appropriate to say. When she failed to think of anything encouraging to offer, she asked, "So where's Mother?"

"There was an accident in the silk mine. She had to go to the healing house last night."

"Really? What happened?" she asked, keenly and morbidly curious. Silk mining was a dangerous job. People slipped on the slick wet caverns in the dark, or cut themselves on broken shale, or fell into hidden black ravines. There were also the legends of killer cave monsters hiding in the dark. They were the creatures that supposedly made the valuable silk. Legend had it that they were huge and blind, with legs like spears and massive scissor-like mouths that could snip off limbs as easily as biting into a steam bun.

"I didn't hear what happened," Jamero said with a shrug. "You'll have to ask her when she gets home."

Mildly unsatisfied, Anri left Jamero to his work and made her way through town, past shops opening for business, children carrying deliveries, and carts of goods rolling down the road.

She left the city behind as she made her way down-river and out to the open grassy fields south of town. Here, farms dotted the hills for miles, most of them raising shufflos for meat, milk, and wool. It was to one of these farms that Anri was heading, the largest dairy farm in Silverlake.

A group of children was already gathering around the shufflo enclosure when she arrived, all of them waiting to milk the shufflos and earn a few extra bits for their work. A musty, earthy smell wafted from the trampled muddy ground on the other side of the gate. Workers behind the fence were leading shaggy female shufflos into their milking stalls while black flies buzzed in the surrounding air.

"Wasn't Darvin coming this morning?" one boy nearby asked a girl who was leaning against a fence post.

The girl shrugged, watching the shufflos with a bored expression. "He joined up with Marlo and Quin to go egg hunting."

"What? I didn't know Darvin wanted to be a rider!"

"Well, you know Quin. He can talk you into anything if he wants to."

"I wouldn't mind being a dragon rider," a small boy next to them chimed in. He looked about ten years old. "Don't you think it would be fun to fly everywhere on a dragon?"

A woman was approaching the gate in front of them, dressed in clean, bright clothes too fine to be working with shufflos. The children all turned to face her, respectfully. This was Lady Dara, the owner of the shufflo farm.

Her silver eyebrows raised at the young boy who'd spoken of wanting to be a dragon rider. "And you'd let it eat our animals, too, no doubt, letting it take half of our herd because you're too lazy to grow your own food?"

All the kids shrank back at the sharpness of her tone.

The young boy cringed. "But, all the songs say that dragon riders protect us," he said meekly.

The woman scoffed. She slid the latch aside and pushed the gate open for the children to enter the pen. "There have been no swarms in hundreds of years. They're never coming back. And still, those flying menaces come in to take our breeding stock and milk beasts."

The boy's face fell, and Anri quietly passed him to enter the pen. A row of huge hairy shufflos was waiting in narrow stalls for the children to milk them, flicking their tails and chewing their cud.

Anri found an empty stool and sat down next to a shaggy, smelly shufflo with full udders. The beast turned to regard her with one huge brown eye, then shook its head to dislodge a swarm of flies and continued chewing its cud with a bored expression.

Positioning her pail under the beast, Anri began her work. Creamy milk filled her pail in rhythmic streams.

She was lucky this time. Occasionally she would get a shufflo that didn't like being milked, and she would have to dodge sharp kicks from their back hooves while she worked.

"Do you think it's true, what Lady Dara said about the dragons?" someone whispered behind her.

Anri glanced back to the gate where Lady Dara waited on a stool next to wooden barrels, waiting to collect the milk and pay the children. Then she turned to see who had spoken, a familiar girl with short brown hair. The girl was leaning to the side to look at Anri from behind her shufflo's back legs.

Anri shrugged. "I see the dragons flying out to hunt in the feeding fields. But isn't that what those fields are for? The animals that aren't good for breeding go out there for the dragons to eat."

The brown-haired girl wrinkled her brow in thought.

Anri turned her attention back to milking her shufflo. The first two udders were just about empty, so she shook out her aching fingers and switched to the next two.

"Well, Lady Dara isn't the only one who complains about the dragonholds," the boy in the stall in front of Anri said. "My father says they should learn to grow their own food and raise their own animals to feed their dragons."

"But the green dragonhold is in the Poison Plains," the girl behind her said. "Only green dragons and their riders can survive out there. They can't raise shufflos for food." Anri suddenly remembered the girl's name: Rin. Her parents lived near the river and dyed wool into colorful yarn for cloth-making.

"Then maybe they should earn money for the things they need," the boy argued. "My father says all they train their dragons to do is play games. Why should we feed them when they never do real work?"

"Well, when I become a dragon rider, I'll find out what they do all the time. I'm sure it isn't just playing games. And"—Rin's voice lowered like she was telling a dangerous secret—"I heard rumors that some northern cities see swarmers still. So what if they come back? We'll need the dragons then, won't we?"

"I don't believe it." The boy snorted mockingly. "But wait, you actually want to be a dragon rider?" He turned to stare at Rin. "Hatching day is coming next season. Have you joined an egg-hunting team?"

Anri turned to regard her as well. She knew a lot of kids were teaming up to search for eggs, hoping that they'd find one and earn a place on the hatching ground, but she hadn't known that Rin was planning to hunt for an egg. If she was here, milking shufflos in the morning with the rest of them, didn't that mean her family needed her working? How would she be able to leave them if her team found an egg?

"Of course. Joining a team is my best chance of finding an egg and making it to the hatching ground."

"But . . . why?" Anri blurted. In her distraction, she forgot to keep milking. Her shufflo grunted and stomped a back hoof threateningly. Anri turned back to her work before Lady Dara could notice her slacking.

"Who wouldn't want to be a dragon rider?" Rin said with a sigh. "Just imagine being able to fly all over Avria, to join in the dragon games—not that that's all they do, I'm sure—and to have a dragon friend for the rest of your life!"

"But . . . doesn't your family need you here?"

"Well, if I go to the hatching ground, they won't have to feed me anymore."

The boy in front of them snorted. "Except the dragonholds get all their food from the villages."

Rin narrowed her eyes at him. "And when I get chosen by a dragon, the hold will give them money every season. Didn't you know that?"

"What?" Anri asked, turning back again. "The dragonholds give money to the families of riders? Really?"

"Really, Anri! If you started talking to people more,

you'd learn so much!" Rin rolled her eyes and stood with her full milk pail. "Remember Nader? His family lives in the house next to ours. He bonded with a red dragon last Hatching Day, and his family gets ten silver marks every season now that he's a rider. I've seen him bring it to them."

"He does?" Anri whispered, trying to imagine so much money.

"That's right. Now, if you'll excuse me, I have some egg hunting to do!" Rin hauled her pail of milk out of the pen and took it to Lady Dara to collect the copper bits for her work, leaving Anri sitting in stunned silence.

Ten silver marks! That would more than cover all the money she made. It would even make up for their lost customers since Father died. Then Jamero could focus on learning his craft without worrying about losing customers.

Why had she never heard of this before? In thoughtful silence, Anri finished milking her shufflo. When the pail was full and the shufflo's udders were empty, she carried the milk to the gate to collect her copper bits.

With her mind circling around the ten silver marks, Anri made her way to Elder Ronard's cormant farm at the bottom of the hill just outside the city. The enormous birds had to be housed downwind of residences because the stench of their droppings reeked so badly most people would rather not breathe at all than have to smell them all the time.

The young birds Anri cared for were too small to stay in the fields with the adults, so it was her job to feed them, water them, and rake the soiled straw out of their stall.

She imagined how much food ten silver marks could buy as she lugged buckets of water from the well. She thought of the tools and rich ore Jamero could buy while she shoveled grain into the trough for the young birds. The colorful, flightless chicks squawked and squabbled over the food. While Anri raked pungent piles of straw into a manure cart, she imagined her mother sleeping until morning instead of having to go to work in the middle of the night. She would wake up feeling rested and would be able to spend more time with her family.

Wiping the sweat from her forehead and neck, and relishing in the fresh air outside, Anri dumped the manure onto a pile that Elder Ronard sold to local fruit and vegetable farmers.

"Good morning, Anri," Elder Ronard greeted as he strolled from his house carrying a mug of steaming hot kaffa. Short prickly grey hair sprouted over his head and chin, highlighted by deep lines showing the age of the respected man.

"Oh, good morning, Elder Ronard. The chicks are all fed and watered, and they have fresh bedding. I think they're getting used to me," she said, proudly. "I didn't have any trouble with them today." The steam from the elder's cup wafted toward Anri, making her mouth water at the spicy-sweet scent.

He gave a quick nod and reached into his pouch to draw out her payment. "Remember that they're still not trained," he warned. "It's best to keep your distance from these birds. They may be small still, but those talons could flay you open like a trout if you aren't careful."

"Yes, Elder." Anri still bore scars on her arms and legs from when she'd first taken the job. The chicks had been much smaller at the time, but they hadn't trusted her as they did now. "Thank you," she added as he handed over three copper bits for her morning's work.

For the next few hours, Anri scurried from job to job. She gathered water for a manor, took a sack of clothes to the cleaners, swept out a walkway, and sorted out bruised fruits.

When she had finally gathered enough money for the things her family needed, Anri took her earnings to the market district. Outdoor stalls lined the streets with people selling everything from jewelry to clothing to toys, and especially food. Young children ran from stall to stall, likely the youngsters of the shop owners. Adult cormants strode patiently through the crowds, drawing carts behind them over the cobblestone streets.

Turning off the main road and into a narrower side street, Anri made her way to her favorite shop. It was run by a man named Jeb, who seemed to be doing well for himself despite the out-of-the-way location. He always had the foods Anri needed, everything was always fresh, and Anri could always count on him to charge fair prices.

"I'll get my usual order," Anri said, dropping her pile of copper coins into the small clay dish on his table. She fidgeted anxiously. Her stomach was snarling with hunger, and she knew her little brother would be awake by now.

Behind the counter, Jeb took a bite of his apple, wiping the juices from his mouth with his sleeve. He was an older man, with long white hair and eyes that were always half-closed, like he was tired of dealing with everyone's drama.

He grabbed the dish and shook it to separate the coins and count them.

"That's not enough," he grunted.

. . .

To continue reading Anri and the Dragon Quest, visit nadavenport.com/anri-free to claim your free copy.

WEREWOLF MAX

Lost in the Graveyard

Werewolf Max and the Midnight Zombies

Werewolf Max and the Banshee Girl

Werewolf Max and the Monster War

FAIRIES OF TITANIA

The Last Fairy Door

The Dragon Key

The Tree of Worlds

DRAGON RIDERS OF AVRIA

Anri and the Dragon Quest

Secret of the Dragon Egg

Dragon Wings

A Dragonhold Christmas